THE SCIAL EXPERIMENTS
OF *Dorie Dilts*

Dumped
by Popular
Demand

P. G. Kain

ALADDIN MIX

NEW YORK   LONDON   TORONTO   SYDNEY

To Chuck's best friend and mine. W. B. C.

ALADDIN PAPERBACKS
An imprint of Simon & Schuster Children's Publishing Division
1230 Avenue of the Americas, New York, NY 10020
Copyright © 2007 by P. G. Kain
All rights reserved, including the right of reproduction
in whole or in part in any form.
ALADDIN PAPERBACKS and related logo are
registered trademarks of Simon & Schuster, Inc.
ALADDIN MIX is a trademark of Simon & Schuster, Inc.
Designed by Mike Rosamilia
The text of this book was set in Bembo.
Manufactured in the United States of America
First Aladdin Paperbacks edition September 2007
2   4   6   8   10   9   7   5   3
Library of Congress Control Number 2006938520
ISBN-13: 978-1-4169-3519-3
ISBN-10: 1-4169-3519-3

ACKNOWLEDGMENTS

I would like to thank the Trader Joe's company for producing and selling their chocolate-covered, peanut-butter-filled pretzels, because without these treats a day of writing would be much more difficult.

The next best thing in the world, not filled with peanut butter, is William. I'm lucky to have such a wonderful person to go through life with. Thank you for always helping me through any obstacles and sharing in all my successes.

One of the great benefits of writing a book is that you get a chance to publicly thank your friends and family. Thank you to my friends (in order of appearance) Beth, Rebekah, Shari, Sara, Patrik, Pam, Justin, Joe, Chris, Madeleine, Virgil, Loins, and Ellen. Thanks to my family—Mom, Dad, Judi, and Matt—and to my extended family, the Crows, especially Mim.

Thanks to my fantastic agent, Diane Bartoli of Artists

Literary Group, whom I can always count on to be on my side. Thanks to Julia Richardson for acquiring this project and to Margaret Wright for carrying it through to the end with such enthusiasm.

Most of all I want to thank YOU. Yeah, you, the kid who loves to read so much that you are actually reading the acknowledgments. I've been thinking about you for a long time. I'm so glad and grateful to finally have you here. I want you to know how much I truly appreciate you reading this book. I'd love to hear from you, so please stop by my website (www.TweenInk.com) so I can thank you in person.

CHAPTER

"I have never belonged wholeheartedly to a
country, a state, nor to a circle of friends. . . ."
—Albert Einstein

I firmly believe that one day the world will understand
the unspoken cruelty of alphabetized seating charts.
In Spanish class I sat next to Amanda Donohue (my
last name is Dilts) for an entire year. Amanda was one of
the most popular girls at Rancho Viejo Middle School.
Each year her birthday was practically a national holiday.
Her locker was decorated with such ferocious planning
that Martha Stewart would have felt inept. At lunch the
entire cafeteria serenaded her with a jazzy version of
"Happy Birthday." Now, when I say the entire cafeteria,

I mean the *entire* cafeteria. My god, the lunch ladies in hairnets probably sang the loudest. But Amanda wasn't the only girl who got the red carpet for her birthday. Julie Tavner and Annie Dowd were treated the same way on their birthdays. As a point of comparison, the only person outside my family who acknowledged my birthday was my orthodontist, who routinely sent me a Snoopy card with his best wishes and a not-so-subtle reminder to schedule a checkup.

For a full year I sat right next to Amanda. I endured her *moo-chase grace-ee-us*'s and even loaned her a pencil or pen at least once a month. As a point of clarification, I would like to point out that when I say *loaned* I am only referring to the fact that she would say, "Can I borrow?" She would use the word *borrow* but not once was my writing implement ever returned. Not once. Not ever. I didn't care so much about the pencils, but sometimes I would loan her my very favorite pen. Eventually I wised up and started carrying an extra pencil from the put-put course just for her.

Then, as luck would have it, during my sixth-grade spring break my family ran into Amanda's family on the monorail at Disney World. (We were celebrating the fact that my little brother, Gary, was finally tall enough to ride Space Mountain. This, to me, is like celebrating Pamela Anderson's boobs by going to Hooter's, but I had little say in the matter.) At first the coincidence overwhelmed me, but when you consider that a tenth of the families in Rancho Viejo go to Orlando for break and the limited number of monorails and so on, the numbers show a surprisingly high probability of running into at least one person from home. When I saw Amanda, I didn't think. I just let out a big "Ohmygod. Amanda. How are you?"

So after a full year of sitting next to me and treating me like a satellite branch of Office Depot, Amanda looked right at me and said, "Oh, hi." As soon as she uttered the syllables I could tell she had no idea who I was. She just looked at me blankly. I wanted to bolt off the monorail, but before I could, I heard "Please stand clear of the closing doors," and our compartment was sealed like a Ziploc bag as we zoomed toward the Magic Kingdom. Amanda looked at me and said, "Do I know you?" Okay, some people might think she was just being a jerk and *pretending* not to know me, but I assure you that was not the case. Amanda genuinely had no idea who I was. I thought maybe it was the fact that it was so out of context. My

God, we were on a monorail. So I said, and I truly can't believe I said something so dorky, but I actually said, *"Sí."* I thought maybe this would be a fun trigger and she would immediately respond with *"Hola,"* or *"Cómo estás?"* but that was not the case. My *español* only confused Amanda more. The blankness in Amanda's eyes landed on me like a prison floodlight. She was like, *Who is the completely deranged person who seems to know my name but doesn't speak English?* I should have just handed her an invoice for a case of pencils. "Spanish class," I said quickly, and in English. "I'm in your Spanish class." This seemed to help Amanda remember who I was, though I was never sure if she actually recognized me or just did a very good job pretending. Our families made some small talk for a few minutes before the monorail doors opened again and we escaped into the crowd.

To Amanda, I was invisible. I sat next to her every day and she didn't have any idea who I was. I'm not saying she had to know my name, though that would have been nice, but she didn't even recognize me. I wasn't even a blip on her social radar screen, and there wasn't anything I could really do about it. Rancho Viejo is a pretty small town, and I had known most of the kids since school started. Our social positions were pretty much set by the time the snack break ended on the first day of kindergarten. The popular girls went for the Oreos while I opted for the more wholesome Fig Newtons. They immediately found one another and started building the foundation of a clique that would endure long past grammar school.

I was always just a bit of a loner—preferring to read or take a walk near the lake by myself. Popularity never seemed to matter to me. Some girls were popular and some were not. Some girls had brown hair and some did not. It all seemed somewhat random to me. The fact that I wasn't popular was just something I accepted.

Lately, however, I have wanted that to change. I've watched the popular girls from afar for so long and have begun to envy their shopping sprees, slumber parties, and endless gossip sessions. They always seemed to be having so much fun, and they always had someone to hang out with.

I was never a social outcast like the kids that wore black from head to toe and treated their scalps like Easter eggs. You know the kind. They claim to be all anti-everything. (News flash: If you are wearing black because all of your friends are too, it's called conformity, not individuality.) But still, you could always find them hanging out in the parking lot of the Ralph's on Hermosa Street. There were always at least half a dozen of them, so even the freaks had a community.

I guess I could have been part of the nerd community since I love all things scientific and Jane Goodall, the world's foremost primatologist, is like my total idol. I've tried to explain this to my mother by saying, "Mom, she is like my Oprah." I think that finally made it click for her. Goodall is a real scientist's scientist. I've read almost every article she has ever written and that would certainly gain my entrée to the geek social group. Granted, this is only one rung above the absolute bottom of the social ladder, and I am not even sure what's on the absolute bottom. That doesn't even bother me so much. What does bother me is that the nerds are almost all boys. I don't have anything against boys—it's just that introducing a member of the female species to their community would probably make half of them explode and the other half put the exploded bits under a microscope. (Okay, gross but totally true.) I think the closest any of them has been to a real live girl was during a Princess Leia autograph signing at a *Star Wars* convention. This is probably why Jane, Goodall that is, left England to go live with the chimpanzees in

Tanzania. Chimps are easier to deal with than boys and certainly much cleaner.

Of course, I knew infiltrating the popular clique at Rancho Viejo at this late date would be impossible, so when my parents sat me and Gary down for a family meeting a week after school ended, I saw an opportunity.

My parents came into the family room and turned off the rerun of *Friends* Gary and I were watching. "Kids," my Mom said in her I-have-some-bad-news-but-I-love-you-so-much-it-won't-matter tone, "we have some big news." In any normal family this would have been the prelude to the Big D: Divorce. My parents, however, are sickeningly and embarrassingly in love with each other. They think the Post-it note was invented so they could write love notes to each other. They leave them *everywhere*—on the bathroom mirror and the windshield of the car. Even milk cartons were canvases for their affection until I made the fridge off limits. I mean, who wants to open the door of the fridge looking for some leftover spaghetti and find "Janet—You are as beautiful as the day I met you. Your Honey Bear"? Ugh. Not only does it make you a candidate for some serious therapy, but you lose your appetite.

Anyway, with divorce only a remote possibility the news

could have been anything. My Dad took my mother's hand and they both sat down on the couch next to us. My mother was an actress before she became a full-time mom, so she has a tendency to make everything sound overly dramatic. Despite this fact, my mom is the official voice of the parental unit, and all announcements come from her.

She spoke slowly and deliberately. "Your father has been offered a new job. He has been selected to run the new biotech lab at Nelson Science. This will mean greater respon-sibilities for him and more money." Gary and I sat silently. I mean that was great for Dad, but I couldn't see how this would really affect my day-to-day life until the next sen-tence: "Now, this job is in New Jersey, and I know how you both love California, but we'll have to move in a few weeks."

"No way," I shouted. The news shocked me, like when you hear an announcement over the loudspeaker while you are taking an intense test.

"Can I get a dirt bike if we move?" Gary asked. He never missed an opportunity to petition for any number of ridiculous presents from dirt bikes to swimming pools.

My dad finally spoke. "Now, Dorie, don't be too upset. And Gary, we'll see."

I just sat there in silence contemplating the possibilities.

New house. New school. New friends. My parents read my silence as dismay. "Dorie," my dad said, "are you upset?"

"Upset?" I said. "I'm not upset. I'm ecstatic! This is exactly what I needed." I jumped up from the couch, gave both my stunned parents a hug, and repeated, "Thank you. Thank you." It wasn't that I hated Rancho Viejo; I just didn't particularly love it. Starting over in a new school was like getting a chance to begin my life over again, and this time I wouldn't make the same mistakes.

I went to my room, found my lab notebook from biology class, and turned to a fresh page. (I love the way the graph paper covers the surface of the page with perfect little squares.) If I was going to be popular at my new school, I realized, I would need a plan—a foolproof, scientific plan.

When life hands you an opportunity, you need to be prepared to take advantage of it. I decided that when I got to New Jersey, I wasn't going to leave anything to chance. I would make sure I did things that would guarantee my popularity. Finally, I had seen the light. All those years I thought if you were just nice to people and smiled at times, you stood just as much of a chance of being popular as anyone else. How stupid was that?

Popularity is not something that happens to you. It's something that you make happen, and I was determined to make it happen.

Dorie Dilts—June—Lab Report
Objective: To be popular at new school.
Materials: 1 (one) 13 year-old soon-to-be seventh grader of average height and weight. Long brown hair (father) and blue eyes (mother). Skinny, terrible chicken legs but promising bust line. Good skin due to strict adherence to cleansing routine and genetic good fortune. Loves nature, reading, and musical theater and has an exceptional talent for science (if I do say so myself!).
Methods: To be determined.
Conclusions: To be determined.

CHAPTER

2

"The usual approach of science of constructing a mathematical model cannot answer the questions of why there should be a universe for the model to describe."

—Stephen Hawking

I wasn't sad to leave Rancho Viejo, but I did spend some time saying good-bye to all the places I loved. In a canyon not far from our house there was this old craggy tree that looked like it was the oldest living thing in the world. The branches felt stiff and brittle, and looked like the wind had taken decades to get them all pointing in the same direction. I took a picture of the tree with the digital camera I got for Christmas last year.

The sun was setting, so the sky was this soft pink and orange. There was nothing else around the tree, so the sinewy, pale branches stood out in the photo like a diamond necklace against black velvet. I framed that picture and it was the first thing I put up in my new room.

You can buy almost anything online, from autographed sneakers to cheddar cheese, to a whole house. That's what my parents did. They went online, took a virtual tour, showed jpegs of the house to Gary and me, and then they bought the house. My dad said he was glad we were moving to the house rather than the other way around because the shipping costs would have been murder. Of course, they hired a building inspector to make sure the house wasn't made out of cardboard or anything, but the first time we actually stepped foot in the house was the day we moved in.

Our house in Cali was one level and had these huge windows that looked out over a rocky, typically Northern California landscape. Our new house is surrounded by grass, and outside every window is a view of an oak or a maple tree. Gary is in seventh heaven since there is a pool with a diving board in the backyard. My mom keeps calling the new house a "traditional colonial," which basically means it looks like it could have been in one of those really old black-and-white television shows like *Leave It to Beaver*. There are two floors—the top floor has everyone's bedrooms and the ground floor has everything else. At first this was a novelty since we never had stairs in the old house. But after the umpteenth time of being upstairs and needing something downstairs or vice versa, the fun sort of evaporated.

Having lived now for two and a half months in Greenview, New Jersey, I can say that there are definitely differences between the West and East coasts. For example, in California if you go to a restaurant and order something to eat back at your house you say you want it for "take away," but here in New Jersey when I say that people look at me like I'm insane. Here you say you want it "to go." It's a small difference but a difference nonetheless. In Rancho people said things were "mad cool" or "mad busy." "Mad" was basically a way to say "very." Here, "mad" only means "angry" or "crazy."

The week before school started I parked myself at the Starbucks at the Greenview Galleria. There are actually two malls in Greenview, New Jersey. However, mall walkers and moms with screaming babies dominate the Greenview Commons. I figured this out even before my slice of pizza from the Sbarro in the food court was cool enough to eat. I finished my pizza and left the Commons since there was nothing there that could help me. Through the process of deduction I figured out that the Galleria is the teen hangout/shopping mall.

One thing I like about Greenview is that you can either walk or take a bus anywhere. We live only five blocks from a bus line that goes directly to the Galleria. Oh, the freedom of the bus for a teenager cannot be overestimated. Sure, it would be better to have my driver's license and a car, say a lime green PT Cruiser or a purple Volkswagen Bug, but a bus is way better than having to get one of your parents to drive you around.

I got off the bus and entered the Galleria through the food court. As different as some things are from Rancho Viejo, some things are exactly the same. Once you are inside the mall you could be anywhere in the entire country. Every mall has the same big stores at each end with never-ending sales, the same small kiosk vendors selling earrings and imposter perfumes, and a food court with overpriced sodas and not enough places to sit. You'd have to look at the tax rate on your receipt to get even a clue about which state you are in. I mention this because there is no tax on clothes in New Jersey! The stores, however, are exactly the same in almost every mall and must have the same merchandise across the country. Although it's hard to believe the Gap in Miami, Florida, sells as many mittens or ski parkas as the one in Bangor, Maine.

I was not at the mall to shop. I was not at the mall to check out the newest DVDs. I was not at the mall to eat one of those gooey cinnamon buns that are almost impossible to resist. (Okay, I actually did get a cinnamon bun at some point because they are just so freaking good, but that was not my actual purpose for being at the mall.)

I was at the mall for research purposes.

At first my plan was to show up at school next week wearing my favorite pair of old Levis and this orange and blue striped polo shirt that is so comfortable that I've actually worn it to bed a few times. Then as we were eating dinner one I night I realized my mistake. "Duh!" I yelled out between forkfuls of my dad's lasagna.

"Is everything all right, Dorie?" my dad asked. I'm sure he wondered if his daughter was developing an acute case of Tourette's syndrome.

"Fine, Dad. Actually, I just figured something out. Can I be excused?" I asked. My parents saw that I had finished most of my dinner and agreed to excuse me if I promised to do the dishes before bed. I promised and ran to my room. I took out my notebook and crafted my plan. Appearance is an obvious factor in popularity, and clothing is an important part of appearance. If I had any chance of being popular with the kids at Greenview, I needed to find out what the kids at Greenview were wearing. I could *not* let my own personal preferences guide my decision. I needed to use science so that I could make some smart choices. I took out my notebook and filled in one of my earlier TBDs.

Dorie Dilts—August—Lab Report

Methods (revised):

1.) Determine target audience.

2.) Develop spreadsheet for data
   collection.

3.) Observe behavior pattern of target audience.

4.) Gather data and place in spreadsheet.

5.) Use findings to determine most popular
   fashions for Greenview Middle School students.

6.) *Purchase highest-ranking garments for first day of school.*

The Starbucks at the Galleria was an ideal location for the third step of my experiment. It has a seating area at the edge of the food court that overlooks two levels of the mall and enables a clear view of American Eagle, FCUK, and Forever 21, the three most popular stores in the mall. (I know this because I called the Galleria management office posing as a real-estate developer and asked about the stores with the highest sales volume.) I ordered a chai tea latte from the barista and busied myself around the sugars and stirrers until the perfect seat was free. As soon as it was, I grabbed it and opened my notebook. The night before I worked on the first two steps of my project and developed a scoring sheet and a list of qualities my target audience needed. I identified my target audience—girls between the ages of twelve and fifteen shopping with other girls between the ages of twelve and fifteen. Anyone shopping with her mother was out. Anyone shopping alone was out. Anyone who had a bag from the dollar store on the upper level was out. My sample had to be very select.

Once I identified a target, the rest was easy. I simply took note of her behavior in the store. Actually purchasing a garment gave that garment one point. If the target tried something on, that gave the garment another point since it meant she was really dedicated to the garment. If the item was on sale and she purchased it, the item lost one point since she might be motivated by value over style. However, if both girls, or all the girls in the group, purchased the same item the point value of that item was multiplied by the number of girls in the group. So if two girls purchased a garment I would multiply that garment's total points times two. If three girls purchased a garment that garment's value would be multiplied by three, and so on, and so on.

When I located someone from my target group, I observed her carefully. I took note of what she purchased and how much she purchased, and wrote down a thorough description of each garment.

For example, at 2:08 p.m. a group of three girls purchased a total of fifteen items at Forever 21. Two of the girls were wearing jeans and the blond girl who looked like the point person wore a very short skirt—or maybe it was a very wide belt, I wasn't sure. Each of the girls had shoulder-length hair that was blown out at the ends in a bouncy curl. All three were drawn to the Pucci-inspired pink or aqua floral prints in the store. None of them even touched the brown floral print. I made a note in the margin of my notebook to do further research on the repellent nature of earth tones. Since they were traveling in a group of three, each garment's final score was multiplied by three.

Each night I went home and organized my research by placing it on a spreadsheet that allowed me to identify the most popular articles of clothing. After the first day there were no clear leaders, but by the middle of the second the most popular items were making themselves known like a streptococcus germ against the red jelly of a petri dish. (Okay, I realize this analogy is a bit gross, but it is quite apt.)

If I had been making my decisions based purely on my own personal preferences, I would have taken the money my parents gave me for back-to-school clothes and bought the soundtrack to *Avenue Q*, which I have been dying to see ever since we have been within a hundred miles of new York City. Instead I went down the list of garments from most popular to least popular and bought as many as my budget allowed. You would think this would feel incredibly confining, like going shopping for a prison wardrobe. But it was actually totally freeing. I didn't have to think for a moment about what to buy. I didn't agonize over each decision. I simply bought what my research dictated. Sometimes you just have to love science. It can be a beautiful thing.

CHAPTER

"Genius is two percent inspiration, ninety-eight percent perspiration." —Thomas Edison

I t is the night before the first day of school and I cannot fall asleep. I am just lying in bed thinking about tomorrow. I think the angle I'll try to play up is how much I miss my friends back in Rancho Viejo. Yeah, I know. I didn't really have any friends back in Cali, at least none worth missing, but there is no reason the kids in Greenview have to know that. I figure I should create a buzz. Let them think I've already been pegged as popular and that I should achieve my rightful standing at Greenview as a matter of course.

I once read somewhere that having a nickname is a sign

of being well liked. Occasionally people called me Dor instead of Dorie, but I never thought this was a condition of my popularity—it was more likely the result of individual laziness. Yesterday I stood in front of the mirror and practiced my introduction over and over. "Hi, I'm Kiki . . ." Then I'd stop short. I'd smile softly to myself as if remembering a private joke and say, "Sorry, I mean I'm Dorie. Kiki is just a nickname a few kids, actually *a bunch* of kids used to call me back in Rancho Viejo." After literally an hour of practicing and staring at myself, I think I finally got it down. My poor mother believes I have a new imaginary friend as at least twice she called from the kitchen to ask, "Dorie, who are you talking to?" and I kept having to answer, "No one, Mom."

I realize I should focus on trying to get some sleep since big bags under my eyes will not really catapult me into the upper echelons of popularity, but instead I keep saying in my head over and over, "Hi. I'm Kiki. I mean . . ."

My alarm clock rings at six thirty and for just a few seconds I forget where I am and think I am back in Rancho Viejo. After waking up in the same place for so long it takes a while for your sleeping brain to catch up with your waking mind.

At the new house I have my very own bathroom. It's

amazing. The walls are covered in clean white tile, and there is even a bathtub. My mother has decorated the entire thing with these cartoon frogs, which I think are a little juvenile, but at least I don't have to worry about Gary pounding on the door or about stepping on one of his bathtub battleships. I indulge myself and take an incredibly long shower using only the organic soaps and shampoos I bought at an all-natural boutique near Berkeley. I dry and style my hair using the new blow-dryer from Target that I purchased with some of my back-to-school money. After three attempts at blowing out the ends of my hair into bouncy curls I decide I'm as close as I'll ever get.

With my towel wrapped around my body, I step out of the bathroom and open my closet. There it is on the same hanger I had placed it in on the day before: the outfit that took three days and countless spreadsheets to find. Opening the closet, I feel like a NASA scientist unveiling the latest satellite to orbit the globe. Only my closet doors reveal a pair of sand-colored cargo pants with snap-shut back pockets by Miss Sixty and a short-sleeved pink cotton sweater with cute puffy sleeves that an overwhelming 58.7 percent of girls had purchased. Not exactly the solar cell paddles of the Explorer 6, but in my mind just as important.

My parents asked to see what I bought when they finally saw me return from the mall with a shopping bag after three days of coming home empty-handed. I showed them the clothes and I could tell they were surprised by my choices. I'm not really a tomboy, but my relationship to clothing has previously been one of utility. I'm not one of those girls who refuses to wear a dress, but I also don't read *Seventeen* like it's some kind of fashion Bible.

I put on the cargo pants and sweater, and look at myself in the mirror. I like what I see. I wonder why I spent all those years not thinking about what I wore. It's kind of fun to wear cool clothes. I remember the fourth most popular item, a tweed newsboy hat, and dig it out of my closet. I put it on top of my head in a final fashion impulse and make a mental note to go online later and look into a subscription to *Seventeen*.

When I get downstairs my parents are waiting with Gary and the digital camera is on a tripod. "C'mon, Dorie. We don't want you to be late on your first day." The dreaded first day of school photograph. For some reason, I thought maybe the move might have somehow made my parents forget about this embarrassing tradition.

"Do we have to?" I protest before making my way all the way down the stairs.

"Absolutely. Now I have everything all set up, go stand in front of your father, next to Gary." I walk past the dining room table, which my mother has laid breakfast out on, and stand where she has directed.

"You look so pretty, baby," my dad says as he buttons the coat of his brand-new white lab coat. He has to wear a white lab coat to work at his new job. The old lab was very relaxed, and he could basically wear anything he wanted. I actually like the white lab coat. It makes him look important.

"Thanks, Dad. You look like a mad scientist." He laughs and walks toward me pretending to be Frankenstein's monster. My dad can be such a goofball. I love that about him . . . when we are safely behind closed doors. In public, I admit, it can totally embarrass me.

"Okay," my mom says, and I hear the slow *beep beep* as she scurries next to my Dad. Then, the quick beeps. My mom says, "Smile!" The flash pops. And it's over. Only 364 days until the next one.

We eat breakfast quickly even though I can walk to school and don't have to worry about catching or missing the bus. I take a small bite of toast, finish my juice, and grab my backpack. "Bye," I say as I head toward the back door.

"Wait. Wait," my mom says as she gets up from her chair. "You need a jacket."

"It's like seventy degrees outside. I don't need a jacket." My mom walks past me ignoring my protest and grabs my hooded EMS rain jacket from the hook by the door. "I just heard the weather report on NPR. It is supposed to rain later, so you might need this." She holds the jacket out for me to take.

"But Mom . . . ," I whine. Yes, I'm actually whining. What can I say? It's basically a teen impulse to being told to do something you don't want to do.

"Dorie, dear, this is rule number three thousand four hundred twenty-two, section two, paragraph eight of *The Good Mother's Handbook*. When child is leaving house during potential rainfall, insist that said child wear appropriate clothing. Sorry, Dorie. It's in the book."

My mother is constantly making up rules from *The Good Mother's Handbook* as a way of getting Gary and me to do what she wants. I almost always surrender.

"Fine," I say, taking the coat from her. "But I'm only carrying it until it's actually raining."

"That should be fine," she says. "But I'll have to call an approval into the main office so that it's official." She kisses me on the forehead, and I head out the door.

As soon as I am away from the house I take out my iPod, navigate to my FirstDayatGreenview playlist, pop the buds into my ears. The very first song on the list is "Popular" from the musical *Wicked*. Kristin Chenoweth sings the role of Glinda the Good Witch who teaches the Wicked Witch how to be popular. I love this song and don't think I could find a more appropriate selection for today. This song is followed by a bunch of Vanessa Carlton songs and some old-school Madonna.

The first day of school is always traumatic, but the first day of school at a *brand-new school*, that's just off the charts. I should be a bundle of anxiety, but I'm actually more excited than nervous. This will be a new start. No one at Greenview knows I won the science fair in sixth grade with the highest point total ever earned in the history of the science fair. No one knows that from third to sixth grades I ran an annual campaign for the position of classroom rep and lost every election. No one knows anything about me. I have to believe this is a good thing.

I walk down the road our house is on, past a few houses that look a lot like our house. The road we live on, Steeplechase Lane, is lined with huge oak trees that create a green canopy over the entire street. I think about how beautiful the trees will look once fall arrives. Having lived my whole life in Cali, I've never actually experienced a real fall. I turn at the end of the street on to Garretson Road. School is only a few blocks north. I keep walking and practice my whole "Kiki" bit. "This will work," I tell myself. The excitement and the fact that Madonna's "Ray of Light" is playing on my iPod make me pick up my pace.

Finally, I'm in front of the school, and for a few moments I just observe. Greenview is a three-story brick building that must have been built in the 1960s. There is a wide set of steps that leads to the main entrance, and this is where most of the kids are hanging out. Before I go any farther I stop to put my jacket in my backpack and take out my small compact mirror. I adjust the newsboy cap and examine my mouth in the tiny mirror to make sure there is no orange juice pulp stuck between my teeth. Then, in the corner of the mirror, I see a group of girls headed toward me. I safely observe them using my compact as a rearview mirror. These are obviously the popular girls. There are probably half a dozen of them, but three really seem to stand out as the leaders, because the other girls are all directing their attention toward them. The girl in the center of it all looks like a blond, less developed, Lindsay Lohan. She is very pretty and clearly the leader of the group. I totally recognize her from the mall. I take a closer look and realize she is wearing the same exact outfit I am.

I snap the compact closed and smile to myself. "Well done, Dorie," I say out loud. This is going to be so easy. I can barely believe it. All of my research is going to finally pay off. How easy was this? I knew if I just did the research, gathered the data, and made the appropriate calculations, I would see some results. I'm actually wearing the same exact outfit as one of the most popular girls in the school.

OH MY GOD!

I'm actually wearing the *same exact outfit* as one of the most popular girls in the school. The terrible, terrible reality of what I have done finally hits me. I won't be greeted with open arms; she'll trip me on my way into the building. What was I thinking? No one wants to be seen in the same exact outfit as anyone else.

OH MY GOD!

I suddenly remember watching an *I Love Lucy* marathon with my mom and laughing hysterically over an episode where Lucy and Ethel wear the same dress to some event and wind up literally tearing the clothes off of each other.

This is bad. This is *so* bad. This is parents-showing-up-at-the-school-dance bad. It's tampon-flying-out-of-your-purse-to-land-on-the-teacher's-desk bad. I look back up the road and consider walking home, changing, and coming back to school. That would take at least an hour and my mother would freak out about me missing the first day assembly. Just then the school bell rings loudly.

Brrriiiing. All of the kids start moving toward the big doors. What can I do?

Think, Dorie. Think.

I seriously consider taking off the pink sweater and just going to school in my bra. While this might make a very strong fashion statement, it is also almost guaranteed to get me expelled, and homeschooling leaves very little chance of being voted most popular. I put my compact back in my backpack and see the jacket my mother made me bring. Quickly I take it out of my bag and put it on. Great. These are my options: I can either keep the jacket on and be called the school Unabomber or take it and the sweater off and be Christina Aguilera. It's almost seventy degrees and it's only eight in the morning, but I don't see any other solution. The second late bell rings and I zip up the jacket and run toward the entrance.

All of the seventh graders file into the smaller auditorium for seventh-grade convocation. We never had any type of convocation at Rancho. Classes just started. Greenview gets each class of students together for a few inspirational words to get the school year started off on the right foot. A few members of the marching band are on stage playing the theme from the movie *Rocky*. The trumpets are so loud I feel like I am standing right next to them even though I am lingering by the back doors. Groups of kids find seats together. They are all talking and laughing with one another. I feel a sudden longing. I really want to be a part of one of those groups.

For now, I try to be as inconspicuous as possible. I take a seat in the far back of the auditorium. The woman I assume to be the principal is on stage with a few teachers. The band stops playing (thank God!), and the principal taps the microphone a few times and says, "Welcome. Welcome, everyone, students, teachers, and staff!" Everyone cheers and yells. The raised level of excitement is beginning to worry me as it means the already warm auditorium is only going to get warmer. I consider just unzipping the jacket a bit but the pink color of my top is so intense that even only unzipping the jacket would reveal my outfit. I scan the auditorium for the girl I saw wearing the same outfit as me. I can't seem to find her so I relax for a second and try to cool myself down by pulling at the elastic cuffs of the jacket and forcing some air in.

The principal continues. "I would like to introduce class president, Holly McAdams." I strain my neck around the column I have chosen to hide myself behind at the back of the auditorium since class presidents are almost always some of the most popular kids in school. There on stage is the girl from my compact mirror, the same girl from the mall, the pretty blonde in the same exact outfit I'm wearing. I shrink down in my seat hoping a small crack will open up underneath me and swallow me whole.

"Welcome back, everyone," Holly says from the podium as she waves to the crowd. I look around the auditorium and I can tell everyone likes her. A few different groups of people give her shout-outs from the audience. Holly is definitely pretty, but she is not the most beautiful girl at school. The thing about her that strikes me the most is her smile. She has this warm smile that radiates confidence. I think for a moment about bringing my camera to school to take a picture of her smile so that I can study it more closely.

I stare at her up on the podium and think, *You, Holly McAdams, are going to be my friend this year no matter what it takes.* I focus on that thought for just a moment until I add, *Unless I die from heat exhaustion in the next few hours.*

The temperature is definitely rising in the auditorium. As Holly gives her welcoming speech I can feel the beads of perspiration forming on my forehead. I pull my schedule out from the front flap of my bag and start fanning myself with it. The tiny breeze does nothing to cool me off. If only I could just take this darn jacket off. It's so hot that my hair is beginning to dampen from sweat. My once bouncy curls are now overcooked pieces of linguini that stick to my face.

At least I am in the back of a dark auditorium. I'll run to the girl's room right after convocation and freshen up before I head to my first class. That way no one will notice that it looks like I just stepped out of the sauna. As soon as I allow this thought to comfort me, I tune back in to Holly's speech.

"And I would like to extend a special welcome to the new students joining us this year. We have three newcomers. Would you please stand up as I say your name? Let's give each kid a big Greenview welcome." That's nice.

What a fun way to welcome the new students. I decide to give the new kids the biggest Greenview welcome I can give until I suddenly realize I don't have any idea what a Greenview welcome is because I am in fact a *new* student. I will be getting *my own* Greenview welcome. The entire grade is going to think they are welcoming Ted Kaczynski to their graduating class.

OH MY GOD.

"From Churchville, Alabama, please welcome Tommy Finch," Holly chirps from the podium. A skinny boy covered in freckles stands up reluctantly. He smiles shyly and the auditorium erupts with, "GREENVIEW HU RAH, RAH HU RAH!" Poor Tommy is so startled by the thunderous noise that he jumps and a few kids laugh at him. I'd give Tommy a friendly smile, but I have my own problems at the moment. In a few seconds I am going to be introduced to the entire class looking like a drowned raccoon as I am sure whatever eye makeup I did have on has melted down my face. I consider the bra-as-top idea one more time.

"From Cape May, New Jersey, please welcome Katherine Fukushima." A stunningly beautiful Asian girl stands up and waves calmly to everyone and once again the crowd goes, "GREENVIEW HU RAH, RAH HU RAH!" Holly smiles brightly at Katherine and even gives her a small wave. Katherine is going to be one of the popular girls, and Holly can recognize this about her immediately.

This is it. I seriously consider just running out of the auditorium, but then I realize that Holly will still announce my name, only I won't be there, and then the principal will call my parents, and the teachers will start looking for me, and I don't know any good places in the school to hide yet, and . . .

"And all the way from Rancho Viejo, California," Holly announces, and I send up one last prayer that she says someone else's name, "Dorie Dilts." I stay seated for a second and wipe some of the excess sweat from my brow but it does little good in altering my appearance. I am covered in sweat. I look like I just lost an immunity challenge on *Survivor.* I stand up slowly at first and then realize I'm only delaying my humiliation and snap to my feet. The sudden motion causes some of the sweat from the back of my head to spin off and I'm sure it must have landed on someone, which is so gross that I don't even look up. The crowd gives its final, "GREENVIEW HU RAH, RAH HU RAH!" I try to smile, but I really just eke out a sheepish kind of grin. Before sitting back down I catch a glimpse of

Holly on the stage. She's not exactly horrified by me, but she does look at me like I am clearly the new strange girl. Her reaction is not nearly the welcoming wave Katherine Fukushima from Cape May received.

I look down at the floor, sit down in my seat, and sweat rolls down my neck.

Twenty-three excruciating heat-filled minutes later convocation ends. Even though we are supposed to go directly to our first period class, I exit the auditorium and head out the main doors to get some air. Luckily no one sees me. Once I am safely out of view, I peel off my jacket. The pink sweater I was once so happy with is now soaking wet and sticks to my body like Velcro. I air myself out for a few minutes. There is no way I can keep this up for the whole day. I will die. They will call my parents during fifth period algebra and explain that their daughter just passed out and died unexpectedly. I'm so hot that I decide to actually take off my jacket for the rest of the day, but when I look down and see how soaked the shirt is, I realize there is no possible way I can walk around school looking like this. The jacket must stay on. I take one last breath of air, determine that the temperature has reached at least a balmy eighty degrees, and head back into the building.

CHAPTER

4

"Nothing shocks me. I'm a scientist."
—Indiana Jones

Every single teacher in every single class asks if I am hot wearing my jacket and suggests taking it off. Each time I smile at them and shake my head no. I can only imagine what they think of me. My God. They see this new girl obviously sweating her butt off yet insisting on wearing her jacket while the late summer sun shines brightly outside. Most of the teachers get the hint to leave me alone, but Mr. Evans, my new Scientific Inquiries teacher, is not so easily persuaded.

When my parents registered me for school, I heard that Greenview had a brand-new science lab that was donated by a local pharmaceutical company. I was totally excited since the facilities at Rancho were basically a joke. I swear the periodic table we used was missing some of the more recently discovered elements.

I walk into the brand-new lab, and it is stunning. There are computers and sinks at every lab station, and smooth stainless steel countertops reflect the overhead lamps. In the cabinets against the walls are microscopes, dissecting boards, and a complete array of chemical compounds. The lab even contains a row of cages for some adorable hamsters and guinea pigs. For a second I wonder about their fate but convince myself that they are there for some animal behavior studies. Just looking at everything makes me smile, but then I remember that I don't want to come off as too much of a geek, so I wipe the smile from my face and pretend to be as bored as everyone else.

I try to find a seat near the window since even the slightest breeze will help minimize my agony. Unfortunately the window is closed. I go to open it before the bell rings, but before I can Mr. Evans taps me on the shoulder. "Those windows are sealed shut due to the new ventilation system, which isn't working too well today."

"Oh, okay," I say, and shrug the whole thing off like it's

no big deal. Who cares that I've sweated off eight pounds since convocation this morning? Scientific Inquiries is my last class of the day. If I can just get through this I can then run home, take off this stupid jacket, and take a shower.

"Welcome to our brand-new lab," Mr. Evans says. He is about as tall as he is wide and has a thick brown beard. He looks like a teddy bear, and you can tell right away that he is one of those teachers who just loves teaching. Some teachers are so obviously in it for the summer vacation, but Mr. Evans is the kind of teacher who counts down the days until summer vacation is over. He is as excited about the new lab equipment as I am.

"This lab was a generous donation from Bradish Pharmaceutical," he says, and then pauses uncomfortably. He coughs and adds, "Bradish Pharmaceutical, making today better and tomorrow brighter." The other students laugh, but I am just in shock. It's one thing to watch a movie and see Brad Pitt drink only Pepsi-brand beverages, but it's another thing entirely when your science teacher has to plug a local corporation.

Mr. Evans begins to go over the course materials, and I grab the bandanna I found at the bottom of my backpack. I make sure no one is looking, and then I quickly wipe my forehead, and then hide the bandanna in my pocket. After eight periods of doing this, I think I've gotten the technique down pat. However, on my fourth bandana wipe Mr. Evans catches me. He looks down at his seating chart and says, "Excuse me, um, Dorie, is it?" I nod my head knowing what he is going to ask. "Would you like to take your jacket off?"

"No, I'm fine thank you." I've noticed the quicker I get the words out, the more likely they are to leave me alone, but this technique does not persuade Mr. Evans.

"Dorie, it is 28.7 degrees Celsius outside, 83.7 degrees Fahrenheit, and I won't go into the degrees Kelvin until later in the semester, but surely you must be roasting."

"No," I say, and show him a desperate smile. "Really, I'm fine." Where the heck is that rainstorm my mother was so worried about this morning?

"Are you sure?" he asks. Oh my God. Why won't he leave me alone? He seems like a nice enough guy, but why is he harassing me about this? The other kids are beginning to pay attention to our exchange. The girl next to me who has had her head down on the desk since the class began turns onto her other ear and says to me quietly, "Just take it off, already."

I ignore her and Mr. Evans continues his line of questioning, "Why would you want to keep it on when it's so warm?"

I believe he actually wants a response so I say, "Ah . . . ah," stammering while I think of something to say.

Then from the back of the room I hear, "Hey, maybe she's trying to smuggle out some of the lab hamsters. You better give her a strip search." This makes the entire room explode in laughter.

I turn around to see who delivered the comment. A boy with shaggy blond hair and sparkling blue eyes is laughing while his friends pat him on the shoulder. He looks like he just stepped out of an ad for American Eagle, but all I can acknowledge is that this jerk has gotten the entire class to laugh at me on my first day of school. What a complete and total ass. I give this guy such a dirty look I think lasers will pop out of my head.

Instead of letting him get the best of me I get in on the joke. "Yeah, that's it," I say. "I've got a hamster circus at home, and we're missing a trapeze artist. Of course, we always need clowns if you want to join," I say, directing my focus at the jerk.

The class lets out an "Ooowww." Score one, Dorie.

Mr. Evans tries to quiet everyone. "All right, that's

enough. Grant, I imagine if you focused as hard on your lab reports as you do on your wisecracks you would be earning much higher grades."

Grant bows his head and some of his shaggy blond hair falls in his eyes. He almost looks like a different person from the cocky prankster willing to humiliate me in front of the class. He seems shy, almost vulnerable, and this makes him even more attractive. Of course, I imagine this is a side of Grant I will rarely see. For the moment he is holding the position of the biggest jerk at Greenview.

I sweat through the rest of the period and count off the minutes until the final bell rings. I walk quickly out of the building, trying to avoid making eye contact with anyone. As I turn down the hall to the main doors, I spot Holly and her friends hanging out by the lockers. She looks great in my outfit. Well, actually her outfit. Instead of walking past them I turn around and head out the side entrance. I take a deep breath and realize a long shower is only a short walk away.

Of course, my mother is waiting for me when I walk in the door. I am desperate to avoid her questioning so I beat her to the punch. "Hi, Mom," I say before the door is completely open. Then I start a rapid stream of statements as I

walk across the kitchen toward the stairs to my room.
"Greenview was fine. Classes are fine. The kids seem nice.
I'm going up to take a shower. I'll tell you the rest later.
Love you. Bye." My mom is not sure what hit her, and I
have made a clean escape. I go into my bathroom, turn the
water on, peel off my clothes, and step under the cool
water. It feels wonderful, like I haven't taken a shower in
weeks.

As the cool water splashes across my face, I consider the
details of my failed experiment. A good scientist learns
from her mistakes. What I need to do is gather more data.
Holly McAdams is clearly the most popular girl at school.
If I narrow my focus and figure out what makes Holly and
her friends so popular, I'll have a better chance at meeting
my objective. I rinse off one last time and grab a towel
from the hook by the door. Before I even change into
clothes, I go to my lab notebook and begin plans on the
next phase of my experiment.

CHAPTER

5

"The best way to get a good idea is to get a lot of ideas." —Linus Pauling

New Jersey is full of diners. There are six in Greenview alone. In Cali, the only diner I remember was a few towns over and hardly anyone ever went there. Here, the diners look like they are left over from that old TV show *Happy Days*, and on the weekends they are mad busy during breakfast. My dad already has a favorite— the Neptune out on Old Highway 31. Personally, I find the red, plastic booths almost unbearably uncomfortable, but my dad thinks the art deco details on the pressed metal walls are "rad." I don't have the heart to tell my dad that the last time anyone used the word "rad" was on *The Cosby Show*.

My dad gets excited when he spots an empty booth by the window. We sit across from each other and open the menus, which are almost the size of a small refrigerator. I'm glad to have some private time with my dad since my mom and Gary are at a soccer game.

The waitresses at the Neptune wear actual waitress uniforms like you might see on Halloween. One waitress is carrying a pot of coffee, and when she comes to our table she doesn't say anything—she just turns over our coffee mugs and pours the coffee. She doesn't ask us if we want coffee or even say good morning. She just turns, pours, and leaves. In Rancho you couldn't look at someone without hearing their life story. New Jersey is all business, and my dad finds this fascinating.

"Did you see that, Dorie?" he asks. "She barely looked at us." He laughs and shakes his head. He's not upset with the lack of formality; in fact, he loves it. My father values direct communication over pretense. I imagine this is one aspect that makes him a good scientist. The waitress returns and takes our order. We both get two eggs scrambled with bacon, whole-wheat toast, and OJ. I decide to get my dad's advice before he gets too focused on his food. I figure I might as well use the resources I have access to.

My dad runs a lab that tests and develops new drugs for a variety of diseases. When he first started out, he worked on a medicine for people suffering with asthma, and he even has a few patents under his belt.

"Dad, I have a question for you," I say.

"You do?" my dad asks, and a look of worry flashes across his face.

"It's okay, Dad," I say to relax him. "It's not about boys or sex or anything."

"Phew," my dad says, and takes a sip of coffee.

"It's about your work."

"Immunology? What do you want to know?" He pours some more milk into his coffee and takes another sip.

"I was wondering . . . when you start working on a new drug for something, what's one of the first things you do?"

My dad puts his coffee down and leans back in the both. He thinks very seriously for a few minutes. I knew if I asked my dad he would take me seriously. A lot of parents would just blow off the question or give some inane immediate response or, worse, answer the question with a question. My dad thinks for a while before answering.

"Well, Dorie, I think the first step of any good scientific breakthrough is a careful and thorough examination of what is already out there. In the lab I try to gather as much information as I can about the disease I'm working against. How does it manifest? Who does it affect? What are its symptoms? A good scientist has to know what he is working with before he makes a serious plan of action."

"Dad!" as soon as I hear his last sentence I shout at him, and he realizes his error.

"I'm sorry. I wasn't thinking. I mean a good scientist has to know what *she* is working with."

"That's better," I say. I know my dad isn't sexist. Sometimes he just forgets how sensitive I am to automatically assuming a scientist is going to be *HE*. It's the twenty-first century, so give me a break.

That night, as soon as I am done with my homework, I start working on my plan. I have dedicated a brand-new notebook to my project. Keeping all of my information in one place will allow me a more concentrated focus. I open the notebook and write HOLLY MCADAMS in big block letters. Underneath her name I write: EASY, CONFIDENT SMILE. I put my pen down, go to my bathroom mirror, and give myself the biggest smile I can. I stare at myself for a few seconds, holding the smile tightly. Eventually my cheeks hurt. That smile was too intense, too Bozo the

Clown meets Botox. I try another smile, a softer, more relaxed one. My lips barely part and the edges of my mouth have the slightest upturn. I stare at myself until I realize the face I'm making looks like I'm constipated and that I'm enjoying it. Well, that won't work.

I go back to my notebook and stare at Holly's name for a few seconds, and then I realize I'm not paying attention to what my dad said back at the diner. I need to look at how the disease affects a group. Sure, Holly may seem like the most popular girl at school, but I need to find out who the other popular girls are and what they have in common with one another. If only one person is afflicted by something, it isn't a repeatable, verifiable condition. I had never though of popularity as being like a disease before, but the more I think about it, the more it makes sense. Popularity is certainly something you catch from someone who already has it, and if popularity is the disease, I don't want the cure.

CHAPTER

6

"Not everything that can be counted counts; and not everything that counts can be counted." —Albert Einstein

When Jane Goodall worked with her first group of primates, she was able to understand their relationships by figuring out who cared for whom. She established social networks by observing groups of primates that shared food or helped each other with grooming tasks such as picking the lice out of each other's hair. I imagine lice won't be much of an issue at Greenview, but I decide careful observation will help me identify the most popular girls. I keep my notebook with me at all times for the next two weeks. I figure

Holly is obviously the most popular person at the school. Even the most cursory observations would determine this. I need to find out who Holly hangs with. This turns out to be easier than I think it will be.

I'm walking up the stairs of the main entrance and I see Holly with another girl, Alexis Martinez, who I recognize from my English class. Alexis seems like a sweet girl, and the fact that she thinks Shakespeare and Dickens wrote at the same time is really more a testament to her imagination than to her intelligence.

Alexis and Holly are standing on the steps just talking to each other. After having observed Holly for about a week, I realize that just seeing her talk to someone is not really a strong enough factor in determining the person's relationship to her. Holly talks to everyone—nerds, jocks, teachers, janitors. I even saw her laughing over a joke with the school nurse once. Really, who laughs with the school nurse? So when I see her talking to Alexis I decide to write it down, but I don't think it will be a determining event until I realize what Alexis is wearing. She has on the same exact pink sweater that Holly and I wore on the first day of school. I watch as Holly chats with Alexis, and at one point Holly adjusts the puffy sleeve of the sweater. Bingo. I mean, it's probably lint instead of lice but who cares? The result is the same.

I decide to walk by very slowly to see if I can hear a snippet of their conversation. A lot of kids are walking past them so I should be able to sneak by unnoticed. I start my slow crawl up the stairs. I make sure I am on the other side of the stairs so I don't seem so obvious, but as I get farther up the stairs I realize that I am too far away to hear anything, so I start moving diagonally across the steps.

Warning: Walking diagonally across a crowded staircase is something you should *never* do. I learned this the hard way. Other people do not expect someone to walk in a diagonal line across a flight of stairs. They are not prepared for it. It's like brushing a cat's fur the wrong way. Of course, at that moment I do not know this, so I just walk closer to my target, causing a few kids to actually trip over me and one poor boy to actually fall on his face. I try to catch him but gravity has too strong a hold of him and he goes crashing down. Everyone on the steps stops to see who has fallen. They all start laughing and I try to help him up.

"Are you all right? I'm sorry," I say. When I look into the kid's face, I realize it's fellow newcomer Tommy Finch.

"Thank you, ma'am," he says in a southern accent as

thick as taffy. He gets up, brushes some dirt off his jeans, and most of the kids who have been laughing leave and go to homeroom. "Y'all sure do move fast here. I better get to homeroom. See ya," he says, and runs away from me as if I might trip him again.

"I'm sorry," I yell after him, but I think he is out of earshot before I get the words out of my mouth.

Holly and Alexis have been laughing so hard at Tommy's big fall that they barely notice me. Once the commotion ends they return to their conversation as intensely as before. As I walk past them I hear Holly say, "See, I told you this would look great on you, too. . . ." I smile and repeat the words over to myself a few times as I head down the hall to homeroom. "See, I told you this would look great on you, too. . . ." I want to get them exactly right in my notebook since I think this will really identify Alexis as one of the most popular girls at school. "See, I told you this would look great on you, too. . . ." I walk past the other classrooms and see poor Tommy Finch sitting in the front of Mr. Ruchlin's homeroom. He still looks a little stunned.

I spend a majority of my lunch periods sitting alone at a table looking over my notes. I don't mind eating alone. I never have. However, I am constantly worried someone will decide to befriend me, sit next to me, and ask, "What are you writing in that notebook?" and I'll be so flustered I'll blurt out my whole project.

I finish my lunch early and decide to go to the bathroom before I head to English. I hate using the bathroom at school, but since I finished my lunch so quickly, I'm hoping the girls' room will be empty. I leave the cafeteria and slowly open the door to the bathroom praying no one will be there. Luckily I have the room to myself, so I take a moment to examine myself in the mirror, but before I can make a full assessment I hear laughter outside the bathroom door. I quickly grab my books and run into a stall.

The door swings open and I immediately recognize Holly's voice.

"And I told my parents that I simply could not live a day longer without a wide-screen HDTV *with* a built-in DVD player in my bedroom. I mean, my God, the one in the media room is all the way downstairs and there is like NO privacy. So, they went to the mall and bought me one this weekend. It's being installed today." There are two other girls with her, and they both respond at the same time with "Awesome." This makes all three of them laugh. I mouth the word silently behind the safety of the stall walls. "Awesome."

I am sitting on the toilet and I open my notebook as quietly as possible to start transcribing the conversation.

"Hey," one of the girls says, "I can bring some DVDs." I think the voice comes from Alexis, and when I peak through the crack in the stall I catch a flicker of the bright pink sweater, which confirms my suspicion. It's definitely Alexis.

"Let's get some really good food like those low-carb popsicles we got that day we had the cookout at the lake," the third girl says. I don't recognize the voice. I write down her comment and as soon as it is in the notebook, I realize this mystery girl must be a close friend of Holly's since they had a cookout at the lake together. But who is she? As the girls keep talking I try to quietly maneuver my head over my knees so I can look under the stall and find out who this girl is. I notice that the top hinge of the stall door is loose so I use one hand to keep the door in place and the other to hold my hair back so it doesn't touch the floor. I strain to get a glimpse of the third girl but all I can see are a pair of pink Skechers. God, what is it with popular girls and pink? I study the shoe carefully and even draw a rough sketch in my notebook since I know this will be the only way to recognize the third member of what I have officially decided to call the Holly Trinity. The school bell rings, but I wait for the girls to leave before I depart from the stall.

As I suspected, once I am out of the bathroom the halls are full of kids going to their next class. Greenview is such a huge school that the halls take on the feeling of rush hour in Shanghai. In a smaller school identifying the popular girls would be so much easier. I quickly look around to see if Holly is anywhere to be seen, and since she is not I direct my attention downward. I'm searching for a pair of pink Skechers as I walk to class. I bump into about a dozen people and a few of them simply move on, but at least a couple of people say something like "Look where you're going!" or "Out of the way!" Usually these comments would upset me, but I'm so focused on my task that I barely register the underscored anger. I search every pair of feet from the bathroom to Mrs. Cobrin's English class, but nothing matches the sketch in my notebook.

In English we're reading Chekhov's *Three Sisters*, which is kind of boring since all the sisters want to do is go to Moscow but they barely even leave their house, which is somewhere in the sticks very far away from Moscow. I constantly want to shake the sisters and say, "Get off your butts and just go already." We are actually reading the play aloud, and gratefully there are not enough roles for everyone so I alternate reading the stage directions with two other kids. This gives me plenty of time to daydream or work on my plan in my notebook. Staring out the window I can see across the small back parking lot to the athletic fields where some kids are playing soccer for gym class. There are three distinct groups on the field. One is really into the game, kicking and passing the soccer ball up and down. Another group is faking it, running along with the ball but not really making contact with it. The third group does not make any attempt to participate. They stand in a clump on the edges of the field and chat while ignoring the soccer ball. As I look more closely at the active group, I notice one of the members is wearing pink footwear, pink Skechers to be exact.

That's her. That must be my mystery girl from the bathroom, but she is too far away for me to confirm my finding. I immediately raise my hand in the middle of Christie Ives reading Olga's speech about how much she wants to go to Moscow. Mrs. Cobrin is not pleased by the interruption. She holds her hand out to stop Christie from reading and acknowledges me with a nod of her head.

"May I go to the bathroom?" I ask as politely as I possibly can.

"If you must," Mrs. Cobrin says with a sigh. I grab my notebook and head past her desk, but she stops me.

"Dorie, I can't imagine what you would possibly need your notebook for in the girls' room unless you are documenting your bowel movements for your physician." This woman is mean. I put my notebook back on my desk and head out the door, and before it closes behind me I can hear Christie picking up where she left off.

There is a girls' room just a few doors down from Mrs. Cobrin's classroom, but I quickly walk past it and head to the doors on the other side of the building that open up to the athletic fields. There I will be able to get a good view of the girl with the pink shoes. I imagine this is a bit how Prince Charming felt chasing after Cinderella. I get to the end of the hall, open the door, and scan the field. I recognize the shoes and am close enough to get a good look. The shoes are attached to a girl I've had my eye on as a potential friend of Holly's and member of the popular elite, Jenny Chang. It was Jenny Chang who was in the bathroom planning a slumber party with Holly and Alexis. I'm not surprised. Jenny is this adorable girl with short dark hair and deep brown eyes. I had a hunch she might be part of the popular clique.

I run back to my English class and thankfully Mrs. Cobrin doesn't even acknowledge my return. At my desk I open my notebook and begin writing.

Dorie Dilts—September—Lab Report
Materials (additional): Holly McAdams,
Jenny Chang, and Alexis Martinez,
aka the Holly Trinity.

"The way to do fieldwork is never to come up
for air until it is all over." —Margaret Mead

Nothing! I hit the enter key on my laptop again
hoping the spreadsheet will reveal a different
outcome, but still I get the same result.
Nothing. I've been observing the Holly Trinity for more
than two full weeks. I have seventeen full pages of observations gathered since September 15. I have done a careful
analysis of each girl's myspace.com page and signed up for
a Google alert for each girl's name in case something new
is posted online. Not to mention that I have spent the past
two weeks of my lunch period eating my bag lunch on my
lap while seated in the same stall of the girls' room where

I first identified the Holly Trinity. So far no one has even cracked the door, let alone have an intimate conversation, while I have been in there.

I'm looking for the one strand that holds their clique together. If I can just unlock this one secret I'll be able infiltrate successfully. If they each knew how to knit, I would simply run into them at some yarn store. If they were all big Coldplay fans, I would start listening to Coldplay and wearing Coldplay T-shirts to school. But there is nothing all three girls have in common. If two girls share something, the third does not.

Holly and Alexis are slaves to the latest fashions. I spotted them shopping together at the mall on four separate occasions during the past two weeks. The last time I observed them they spent a total of one hour and forty-three minutes in Charlotte Russe. After the first hour passed, I was sure I missed them exiting the store. Who in the world spends an hour shopping in one store? My God, I think there are moons orbiting Jupiter with shorter rotations! Jenny, however, was not with them and is known in school for wearing the most outrageous vintage outfits that she puts together herself. On the third day of observation, September 17, she wore an Adidas ringer T-shirt with a denim prairie skirt and pink pillbox hat like Jacqueline Onassis. Anyone else in that outfit would have looked ridiculous, but on Jenny it was stunning and unusual.

Jenny and Alexis are both star athletes. Jenny is on the varsity swim team, and Alexis is the goalie for the girl's soccer team. However, while I was getting my scoliosis checked with the school nurse behind a screen on September 20, I heard two people in the office discussing the fact that Holly holds the school record for missing gym class due to menstrual cramps. The line I wrote down in my notebook immediately after my exam was "Someone should tell Miss McAdams that it's called a *monthly* period not a *weekly*!"

I've assigned each observation an alphanumeric value and placed everything in a spreadsheet. I've developed different algorithms to help me find which characteristics the members of the Holly Trinity share, but each time I enter a new parameter I am met with the same conclusion—nothing. I have to find this missing link. Without it I will be left on the outside looking in. There must be something I'm missing. I try yet another way of slicing the data.

"Nothing!" I say a bit too loudly, and my mom, who is working on her laptop on the other side of the kitchen table, takes notice.

"Dorie, dear, what's wrong?"

"Nothing," I say. "It's just that . . ." For a moment I consider telling my mom the whole plan—how I've made a decision that I am going to be popular at school for once in my life, how I am working day and night on unlocking the secret, how I almost fell asleep during a quiz in Spanish class because I was up so late the night before entering data into my spreadsheet. But I realize I can't when I look at my mom who has been in New Jersey only a few months and already has a group of friends she spends hours with on the phone. A few friends she met at her job writing for the local paper, but others she just met through random coincidences, and now she's the center of a social life. She's even hosting a book club next week. I guess the popularity gene skips a generation because that certain something my mother has, I just don't. Instead of telling her the exact details of my plan, I decide I'll simply let her know the outcome once I have completed my experiment. She'll be so impressed and perhaps mildly surprised when she finds out I am one of the most popular girls in school. For now I'll just be vague. She'll get the hint.

"I'm working on a project and it's just not working out. I think I'm going to have to give up." The thought of spending just one more day eating my lunch in the girl's room is enough to make me throw up. "What are *you* working on?" I ask, trying to change the subject.

"Oh, just a silly article for the paper on ten great recipes for fresh picked apples. It's making me hungry. You want a snack? I was thinking of trying out this baked apple recipe that uses pecans."

"Sure," I say, and close the lid to my laptop. My mom is a fantastic cook. She is always trying out new recipes. In California she sometimes wrote restaurant reviews for the local paper, but here she has been assigned articles about preparing food. Gary threatened to go on a hunger strike after the third day of her homemade sushi research, but everyone in the house enjoyed the work for her "Cookies Around the World" article. I even found a new favorite cookie, the Mexican wedding cookie. Who knew?

My mom hands me some apples from the pantry and instructs me to core them while she works on the nut filling. While we are working, she says, "You know I got really stuck on this apple piece for a while."

"You did?" I ask innocently. It's like my mom knows I don't want to talk about what I'm working on so instead of asking me about it directly she'll find some other way to discuss it. My mom can be relentless, and even though I see right through her little scheme, I am reluctant to stop her.

"Yes," she continues as if my response gave her permission to pursue her agenda. "I was trying to find something new to do with apples. I mean, how many apple pies can a person bake in a lifetime. Yawn, yawn, yawn."

I core the final apple, put the corer in the sink, and jump up on the counter (this is allowed in our house) to sit and listen to the rest of her story. "So what did you do?" I ask.

"You won't believe it, but I went to a used bookstore." For most people this would not be a shocking statement, but for my mother to say this is astounding. She is what is commonly called an early adapter. She had her own domain name before most people had e-mail, her first cell phone was the size of a shoe box, and she is more likely to have her laptop with her than her purse.

"Wow," I say.

"I know. I was waiting for Gary to finish soccer practice, and I saw this cute little antique shop. I had some time to kill, so I decided to go in. In the back of the shop was a huge room filled with old books. I was just wandering around when I stumbled upon all of these old cookbooks.

I started searching through them and found recipes that hadn't been used in decades, some very interesting stuff."

I'm not exactly sure what my mom is trying to tell me. "That's great, Mom, but I'm not exactly looking for recipes."

My mother carefully spoons the nut mixture into each of the cored apples. "Dorie, what I'm trying to say is that sometimes you have to stick with something until a little luck comes your way."

I watch my mom as she arranges the apples in the pan and puts the whole thing in the oven. She's right, and as much as I hate to admit it, she usually is. "Mom," I say, and jump off the counter, "will you make my lunch for school tomorrow?"

"Sure," she says taking off her oven mitts. "But I thought you wanted to buy it."

"I did," I say, "but I think I'd rather buy some time and wait for a little luck."

CHAPTER

8

"Science . . . never solves a problem without creating ten more." —George Bernard Shaw

Eating lunch in the girls' room is not as gross as you would think. Luckily the particular bathroom I am stationed at is just down the hall from the principal's office, so it tends to be extremely clean and infrequently used. On my eleventh day of bathroom duty, I gingerly open the door to the stall as the once-loose top hinge has now almost completely fallen off the door.

I put my juice box on the shelf created by the toilet paper holder and put my sandwich on my lap. (On day three I tried using one of the cafeteria trays, but it got wedged between the wall and the toilet paper holder. I actually had to limbo my way out when the bell rang.) I hang my bag and jacket on the hook behind the stall door and take out a pencil. I've made little lines on the side wall to keep track of the number of days I've been in Stalltown. At first I just did this to pass the time, but now it has become part of my daily ritual.

After I finish my lunch I look at my watch and see that I still have fifteen minutes left until the end of the period. This is pointless. It's been more than two weeks since anyone from the Holly Trinity has even been within earshot of this bathroom. Sure, it was the place where I found them all together, but that must have been a fluke. Criminals return to the scene of the crime, not class presidents. I give up. I decide to go out and get some fresh air before my next class. I take my bag and jacket off the hook on my way out of the stall. But before I can get my backpack all the way on, I hear Holly outside the girls' room shout, "Alexis! Wait, wait!" She sounds pretty far away, and I realize I don't want to be caught outside the stall of the bathroom if they come in here.

I make a break for the door of the bathroom, but the strap of my backpack gets stuck on the hook on the back of the stall door. I thrust my shoulders forward hoping to release the backpack, but instead I tear the door off one of its loose hinges.

Oh my God!

There is no way I am getting out of this bathroom without taking half of the stall with me. The door is tethered to my backpack and swings freely from the one, still attached, hinge. Then I hear Alexis's voice just a few feet from the door. "Holly, Jenny, I just want to be alone."

OH MY GOD!

There is not enough time to release myself from the stall door and make it out of the bathroom unseen. In a split second I decide the only viable option is to go back into the stall. Quickly I move past the sinks, back into the small cubicle. Since my backpack is still attached to the door, the broken corner of it follows me like the eyes in an Uncle Sam "I Want You" poster. I sit down and position my attached backpack on the top of my head so there is enough slack so that the door will close. I use one hand to stabilize the backpack and the other hand and one foot to keep the stall door from swinging open. I can hear the Holly Trinity getting closer. The theme from *Jaws* crescendos in my head.

Just when I get into the perfect position, which would

make a yogi ache with pain, the bathroom door bursts open. Alexis enters crying wildly. Her sobs bounce off the tile walls like Ping-Pong balls. Holly and Jenny are close behind her.

"He's such a jerk. I hate him," Alexis manages to say between her tears. I have to figure out what happened. She seems hysterical. I feel terrible for her. I'd almost offer her a tissue if I weren't using one hand to keep my backpack on my head.

"He's a jerk," Jenny says in support.

"A total jerk," Holly agrees. God, I love how they support one another no matter what. It's truly admirable.

"I mean, you two told me so," Alexis cries. "You both did, and I should have listened to you. You were both right." She sniffles and regains some of her usual composure.

"Well, we had both been there, sweetie," Holly says.

"That's right. Both of us. There and back," Jenny says.

I want to drop the stall door on the floor and jump up and ask, "Where? WHERE? Where have all of you been? Book my ticket on the next flight. I want to go." However, I don't say anything. I sit quietly trying not to think about the lactic acid burning in my arms. The door is so much heavier than I could ever have imagined.

"Holly, Jenny, I'm so sorry I didn't listen to the two of you. I don't know what I was thinking."

"Alexis, you don't have any reason to be sorry. Does she, Jenny?"

"None whatsoever."

"This is something you just had to go through," Holly tells Alexis. I love a pronoun as much as the next girl, but will one of you please use a proper name before the bell rings. Holly continues, "I couldn't tell you *not* to date Grant."

Grant? That jerk from my Scientific Inquiries class? Alexis is crying over that idiot? "If someone had told me what a jerk he was before I dated him, I wouldn't have listened either," Holly says.

"Excuse me?" Jenny chimes in. "Holly *did* tell me and I *still* dated the jerk."

Oh my God. Holly and Jenny dated him too. I might have thought they would have better taste. He is incredibly cute, and I can imagine a circumstance where someone might find him charming, but under the surface the guy is a real jerk.

Alexis has calmed down almost completely and now just sounds a bit sad. "I know it's like old news, but running into him like that just brings it all back. I know I've had the whole summer to get over it, but I still can't believe he dumped me right before summer vacation." He *dumped* her. Ouch.

Through the crack I can see both Holly and Jenny hug Alexis. They are such good friends. I cannot wait to be a part of that group hug. Holly tells Alexis, "Look, it's not you. It's him. The guy is a serial dumper. He dumped me. He dumped Jenny, and he dumped you. He'll find some other sweet girl to date, and he'll dump her, too. He's not worth a second of your time."

Eureka in the bathroom! I have finally found the one thing they all have in common. My elation causes a slight tremor in my already asleep leg, which falls to the ground, but before the door swings open I quickly use my other leg to keep the stall closed. The Trinity has been so concerned with consoling Holly that they have not even come close to noticing me. The bell to end the period rings, and the girls adjust their hair and makeup in the mirror over the sink before heading out the door arm in arm.

Once the door slams behind them, I let my backpack fall from my head and put my leg and arm down. My muscles are so exhausted that I don't notice the stall door falling toward me. It hits me hard on my head and it hurts. For a moment I imagine someone finding me passed out on the floor of the bathroom attached to the stall door. Very *CSI: Greenview*. I consider going to the school nurse for some aspirin, but I am too excited about my discovery to really feel the pain.

All throughout Mrs. Cobrin's class next period I am grinning from ear to ear. I finally found the one thing each member of the Holly Trinity has in common. As Mrs. Cobrin goes on and on about Nora in *A Doll's House*, I imagine slumber parties at Holly's house, shopping with Alexis, and the genuine surprise and appreciation I will show when Jenny decorates my locker for my birthday.

I'm walking on cloud nine as I leave Mrs. Cobrin's class and head to Scientific Inquiries. But as soon as I enter Mr. Evans' classroom, my bubble bursts.

There in the back of the room is Grant Bradish. He is sitting with fellow slacker Doug Hauck, and they are making farting noises by putting their hands under their armpits. How juvenile. Not to mention the fact that if Grant knew anything about air pressure and vacuums he would make a tighter seal to get more sound. I stare at Grant for a few seconds without him noticing me. Grant thinks he is so good-looking that he probably expects girls to stare at him.

I sit down in the front of the classroom and realize what I thought was good news this afternoon really isn't good news at all. This is terrible news. If everyone in the Holly Trinity liked knitting or Coldplay I could fake it somehow, but this is something else entirely. First off, Grant is a complete and total jerk. Second, there is no way in the world that I am going to be able to get Grant Bradish to learn my name, let alone date *and* dump me.

I try to look at the whole thing objectively and start sketching out a few ideas in my notebook before class begins. Could I possibly do it? Maybe it's just a matter of careful execution and determination. Of course, on paper, cold fusion looks as difficult as baking a batch of brownies.

Dorie Dilts—October—Lab Report

Objective: To be popular at new school.

Materials (additional): Grant Bradish. Blond, shaggy-haired potential part-time American Eagle model, part-time stand-up comic, and full-time all-around jerk.

Methods (revised):

1.) Get Grant to learn my name.

2.) Get Grant to date me.

3.) Get Grant to dump me.

CHAPTER

9

"In science we must be interested in things, not in persons." —Marie Curie

I realize my biggest problem in dealing with the Grant obstacle is that I have lost my scientific objectivity. I've let my personal feelings cloud my judgment, and for a scientist this is a major error. Sure, Grant seems like a jerk at school, but I need to become more detached and treat Grant like any other piece of data in my experiment. I decide the best way to do this is to go to the library, gather all the information I can, and start a brand-new file on Grant Bradish. I decide to spend my lunch period in the library.

The library at Greenview is two stories and has it's own wing on the south side of the school. The ground level has a huge table straight down the center of the room and an area for reference questions. The second floor has shelves and shelves of books that create a maze of small study nooks. It's very cozy in a Sherlock Holmes sort of way.

I open the doors of the library and expect to find at least a few kids catching up on some studying, but the place is deserted like a ghost town. I decide to get right to work, so I put my backpack down on the long empty table and head to the reference desk. I recognize the boy behind the counter. It's that Tommy Finch kid from Alabama or some-where in the south. He is shelving some books. I hope he has recovered from my tripping him on the steps a while ago.

"Excuse me," I say very quietly. Just because we are the only two souls in the place does not mean I should ignore the sanctity of the library. "Do you know where the refer-ence librarian is?"

Tommy turns to me, and as soon as he sees me he gives me a big smile like he has never seen another student in the library. "Hey, darlin', what are you doing here?" he asks. His accent is as thick as molasses.

"The library is open, isn't it? I have a study pass," I say, and put my hand in my pocket to dig it out. Maybe the place closes down for lunch.

"Yeah, yeah," he says. "It's just that I'm usually the only chick in the hen house. Y'all eat lunch now. Even the librarians eat lunch now." Tommy seems different from when I have passed him in the halls.

"You're one of the new kids, aren't you?" I ask.

"Yeah. You are too, right? Right nice to meet you. I'm Dixie."

"I'm Dorie," I say. However, I'm confused by his introduction. "I thought your name was Tommy."

"It was. I mean, it is. It's . . . well, some of the jocks have been teasing me because you know I'm *unique*." He says the word with pride, not like it's something he is embarrassed of at all. "They started calling me Miss Dixieland and then just Dixie when they would, like, hit me with a spitball in the halls or something."

"That's terrible," I say. I knew that Tommy had been the source of a lot of teasing since the school year began. He has a lisp and that thick southern accent. He dresses like a runway model from Paris while most of the guys here wear sweats and baseball hats. I thought he was kind of shy but here in the library, away from everyone else, he doesn't seem shy at all.

"Oh, it's not terrible," he says, trying to comfort me. "I

was teased much worse at my old school, and anyway, I kind of liked the name Dixie, so I decided to start using it as my nickname. So call me Dixie, or even Dix. See, I'm going to be famous one day and Tommy is too common. There's already a Tom Cruise *and* a Tom Hanks."

"Are you an actor?" I ask.

"No," Tommy, or rather, Dixie, says plainly.

"What will you be famous for?" I ask.

"Darlin'," he says like he is going to tell me something I should already know, "there are a lot of people who are famous just for being famous. I plan to be one of them."

I laugh out loud but quickly catch myself. After all, this is the library. I like Tommy, I mean, Dixie. I can tell he is not afraid to say or do anything, and that impresses me. The truth is he is already a bit famous here at Greenview, albeit not in a good way, but that's just a matter of perspective. I consider making Dixie my confidant.

"I'm working on a plan of my own," I say slyly to see if he'll bite.

"Ooohhh," Dixie moans in a way that makes me laugh out loud again, and this time I ignore the fact that we are in the library. "So, our Miss Dorie is a girl of mystery. Do tell, darlin'." Tommy opens the half door that leads behind the reference desk and pulls one of the empty librarian's chairs next to his. I just look at the open door and then at Dixie. I think students who don't work in the library are not allowed behind the desk. In fact, I'm sure of it. I hesitate.

"It's all right, darlin,'" Dixie says. "I work here during my lunch period. That way I don't have to worry about getting picked on while the Neanderthals eat their lunch. Sit down and have half my sandwich. It's goat cheese and watercress and simply divine."

I sit and take part of his sandwich. I can't believe I'm eating a sandwich in the library. "So what brings you to the library in the middle of lunch? Does it have anything to do with your plan?" Dix asks.

I tell him everything about my popularity experiment. I tell him how determined I am, how I've identified the Holly Trinity, and how I plan to infiltrate their ranks by the end of the year. I even tell him about my misfire during the first day of school that left me in a pool of my own sweat. He laughs, but it is easy to tell that he is not laughing at me. He laughs with me over my huge miscalculation.

When I'm finally done explaining everything he says, "I love it! It's very *The Trouble with Angels* meets *The Nutty Professor.*"

"Huh?" I say.

"Darlin, they're old movies. We are gonna have to get you a Netflix account." He pours some of his organic passion fruit soda out of the bottle into his glass and takes a sip. I can tell Dix would never drink directly out of the bottle. "Sounds like the Holly Trinity is definitely the most popular clique at school. I don't know that Jenny girl, but everyone knows Holly. I know Alexis a little because I sit next to her in French class." He takes a sip of his drink with his pinkie extended. "Good plan you got there darlin', but I still don't understand what brings you to the library."

I look down at Dixie's glass of passion fruit soda and stare at the carbonation as the gas forces its way to the surface of the beverage. I'm reluctant to reveal the entirety of my plan to someone who is for all intents and purposes a complete stranger. The only person who has any hint of my plan is . . . well, actually no other living person has any idea about my experiment. I decide that if I get hit by a bus I would want at least one person to decode the mystery of my notebooks, and that person might as well be the one sitting across from me nibbling daintily on a goat cheese and watercress sandwich.

"So, what brings you to the library?" Dixie asks a second time.

"I need to find everything there is to know on Grant Bradish. Do you know who that is?" I ask quietly.

"Dorie, you would have to walk around the school headless to NOT know who Grant Bradish is. He is the coolest, cutest, most popular boy at Greenview."

"Yeah, well, I have to get him to date me and dump me before the end of the year." Dixie looks at me like I have just said I need to start a colony of clones on Saturn by the end of the year. "It turns out each member of the Holly Trinity dated and got dumped by Grant. It is the only element that ties all of them together. It's the only thing that can guarantee my popularity with scientific certainty." I explain the smaller details of my plan to Dixie, and he listens very closely. When I finish, a moment of silence passes between us. For a moment I think Dixie will start laughing at me and tell me how ridiculous I am, but instead he says, "So you are here to do as much research on Grant as you can to find out what makes the young heartthrob tick?"

"Exactly!"

"I love it, darlin'. It's very *Frankenstein* meets *An Affair to Remember*."

"Yeah," I say, even though I've never actually seen either of those movies. "See, I've done electronic research, but what I haven't done is look at historical research like old school newspapers and yearbooks."

"Well, I know where those are," Dixie says, and he throws the sandwich wrappers in the trash and grabs my hand. We head out from behind the reference desk, up the stairs to the second level, and all the way to a shelf against the back wall. "Here they are," he says, and makes an elaborate gesture like one of the models on *The Price Is Right* might do to a new car or refrigerator. The shelves contain decades of the *Annum*, the school yearbook, and the *Gazette*, the school newspaper.

"Thanks, Dix. I better get started," I say.

"No problem, darlin'. I'd stay and help you out, but the librarians freak out if they come back and no one is behind the desk. Tell you what, I'll take a yearbook and start looking through it to see what I can find." He grabs last year's *Annum* off the shelf, and I grab the last two years of school newspapers.

I find a study desk in a hidden nook not too far from the shelf, but before I get a chance to even set up some grids in my notebook to help me organize the data, the bell rings. I put the newspapers back on the shelf and take a moment just to look at the well-ordered collection of materials. I smile to myself because I know what I am looking for is somewhere on that shelf.

CHAPTER

After a week of spending my lunch period in the library, I have completely exhausted all of my resources. While eating with Dixie in the library is certainly more pleasant than balancing my sandwich on my lap in the girls' room, I'm concerned that my lack of serious data will put my experiment at risk. With Dixie's help I have found out that Grant has been voted Class Clown for two years running and that he plays baseball, basketball, and soccer.

For a while I seriously considered developing my soccer skills as a way of impressing Grant. I found one of Gary's many soccer balls and started bouncing it around in the backyard hoping to find out I was an athletic savant who simply needed some unstructured exploration to unlock her hidden talents. I thought certainly the years of gym class I have endured only proved to keep my latent talents well hidden. After twenty minutes of kicking and chasing the ball around the yard I finally gave it one last head butt and the ball landed in the neighbor's yard on the other side of the fence. Mia Hamm I'm not.

When I wake up for school on Friday morning I realize my last shot with Grant is to use the only bit of information I have left. As I open my closet to get dressed I feel a sudden pang of guilt. The entire left side of my closet is filled with the clothes I purchased based on my market study at the mall during the start of school. Most of the clothes still have tags on them, and I have promised myself that one day I will take the bus to the mall and return them since I've so quickly reverted back to wearing the same old jeans and T-shirts that I used to wear back in Rancho.

As I walk to school, I start going over in my head what I will say to Grant during science class. Before I can commit too much of it to memory I spot the Holly Trinity in front of me walking to school together. They are almost always together. I can't believe it took me so long to identify them as a unit. I guess it's like the mystery of learning a new vocabulary word. Once you have learned a new word, do you wind up seeing it everywhere because you have just learned it, or because you suddenly are able to recognize it?

The regularity of their social structure is amazing. Holly is always in the center of the group with Alexis and Jenny on either side. Usually one of them will point or look over at someone. Then the other two will look at that person. There will be a short period of contained whispers, and then, like a firecracker that has been set off, gales of laughter erupt from the group. The three of them laugh and giggle frantically until they spot the next source of their amusement, and then one looks, then the other two, then whispers are exchanged, and the whole thing repeats itself. I have no idea what they are laughing at, but their shared enthusiasm looks heavenly.

All throughout the day I carry my lab notebook with me hoping I will find the time to jot down a few notes about what I will say to Grant during Mr. Evans' class. However, each class prevents me from being able to accomplish my goal. In one class there is a quiz and in another we have to work in groups, so it begins to look like my interaction with Grant is going to have to be more improvisational than I planned.

Near the end of the day, right before Scientific Inquiries, I see Dixie in the halls during a class change. I didn't go to the library today for lunch so I haven't had a chance to fill him in on my plan. I wonder if he would be interested in finding out my next step. His head is down as he walks down the opposite side of the hall. I yell out "Dixie!" but he doesn't pick his head up. I say "Tommy!" and he quickly raises his head, gives me a small wave and a smile, then puts his head back down and keeps walking. I notice some of the boys who I have seen tease him before are right behind him and realize he doesn't want to attract attention to himself. Poor Dixie, if only those boys could see how funny and nice he is when he is alone in the library.

I get to Scientific Inquiries as early as I possibly can. My plan is to say something that will really interest Grant so that I can spark a conversation that he will want to continue after school. He is sitting with Doug Hauck in the back of the classroom as usual. My research has uncovered the fact that Grant's family owns the company that donated the money for the new classroom labs. I've tried to think of something to say about this all day long, and since I have not had a chance to really develop anything, I've decided to rely upon my improvisational skills. I look at the clock on the wall and realize I only have a few minutes to say something before Mr. Evans arrives and class begins. I also realize I have been counting on my improvisational skills to kick in and, in fact, I do not have any improvisational skills. All of my skills are the opposite of improvisational. My skills involve procedure and planning. Despite this sudden realization I walk to the back of the room and open my mouth hoping something alluring and fascinating will just pop out.

"Hey, Grant," I say.

"Ah, yeah?" Grant says, looking at me with a mix of confusion and disdain. Immediately I want to turn around, go back to my desk, and hide under it for the rest of the period. In fact, for a moment I convince myself that Mr. Evans wouldn't mind this at all. However, I've started something I've got to finish.

"I just wanted to say that, you know, like, the marble countertops in, like, the lab are, you know, really cool. Your family really knows how to find a good heat-resistant surface that won't stain. My old school had wooden lab tables. Can you imagine? These tables are great."

Grant looks at me. His former expression of confusion and disdain are now colored with a hint of fear. He thinks I am a crazy person and who could blame him? What type of person would compliment the finish on the tables in the lab? What is wrong with me?

"Ah, thanks?" he says with a distinct upturn in his voice in the end like he is asking a question. Like he is asking, *"Is that what you want me to say to leave me alone?"* Doug, who is sitting next to him, literally has his mouth open in shock. The bell rings and I bolt back to my seat and spend the rest of the period with my eyes focused straight ahead so that I don't accidentally turn around and see Grant.

After class I wait until everyone leaves before I get out of my seat and ask Mr. Evans a few questions to delay my departure. I want to make sure Grant, and almost everyone else, has left the building before I venture out into the hallway. Luckily I am the only kid left in the building as I slam the door to my locker and head out the back door. Then I hear from behind me, "Hey, darlin'!" Immediately I recognize the voice.

"Hey, Dixie," I say. "What are you still doing here?"

"I hate the mob scene when final bell strikes. I usually wait it out in the library until things are more civilized.

How is the experiment?" It's amazing how different Dixie is when there is no one else around.

"My experiment is terrible. I just made a complete fool of myself in front of Grant." I tell Dixie the whole story, and he winces when he hears the worst parts. It's wonderful to have someone to confide in, someone who will sympathize with you when things go badly.

"Now," I tell him, "I'm not sure what I'm going to do."

"I have an idea," he says.

"You do?" I say.

"Yes. I was thinking about your predicament and I did a little research of my own. What do the following movies have in common: *Grease*, *Tootsie*, *Clueless*, and *Cinderella*?"

For a moment I try to picture each movie in my head and find their common attribute, but since I have never heard of two of them, I realize I won't be able to come up with the answer. "I don't know," I finally say.

"Two words: Make. Over."

"Dixie, um, I think that's actually one word."

"Darlin', when I'm done with you, one word ain't gonna be enough."

"When I am working on a problem I never think about beauty. I only think about how to solve the problem. But when I have finished, if the solution is not beautiful, I know it is wrong." —Buckminster Fuller

When the phone rings later that afternoon, my mother, who is in the kitchen working on a recipe for vegetable wontons, answers it before I am able to. "Hello?" she says in the polished professional tone she uses for calls without a recognizable number on caller ID. I'm sure it's Dixie. My mother covers the phone with her hand. "Dorie, you have a phone call. It's a girl named Dixie."

"Mother," I say with a significant amount of awe and disgust, "Dixie is not a girl. Dixie is a boy." Of course, once my mother hears the word boy she gets overly excited.

"Oh," she says, almost dropping the avocado she has been holding in her hand. "A *boy*." She says the word "boy" like she has just discovered a cure for cancer.

"Mom, it's just Dixie. Don't get excited. He is not *that* kind of boy." My mom shrugs her shoulders and hands me the receiver. I keep the mouthpiece covered until I am safely in the other room. Luckily, my little brother is at some kind of practice for some peewee sports team so privacy is a possibility. I realize I have not really gotten a personal phone call before, so I don't have a procedure for handling the situation. From what I have seen on television I should most likely be in a crowded closet somewhere in the house.

"Hi, Dixie," I say brightly.

"Hey, darlin'. Are you free tomorrow afternoon? My mom is going to be working at the salon, so we will have the whole place to ourselves."

"The salon?" I ask.

"She works at the Beauty Spot. It's a hair and nail salon in the strip mall by our house. Do you think you will be allowed to come over?"

"Sure. My brother, Gary, has a soccer game, and I was gonna go with my parents and just read a book or study in the car."

"That's funny," Dixie says with a slight laugh.

"What do you mean?" I ask.

"Your joke about studying and reading in the car."

"Oh," I say, not revealing that what I said was not a joke at all.

Dixie and I make plans to meet the next day. He gives me explicit instructions to wash and condition my hair but not to style it or wear any makeup. He wants to start with a clean canvas. I like thinking of my appearance as a canvas. It makes me think that I have endless possibilities.

Of course, getting permission to go to Dixie's on Saturday is easy. I think my parents are secretly thrilled I have someone to hang out with. I follow Dixie's instructions during my shower—I shampoo and condition my hair. Afterward I simply comb through my hair so that I don't get any tangles. I'm sure Dixie thought the temptation to do more visual preparation would be greater than it actually is. Before I leave the house, I jot down my progress in my lab notebook.

Dorie Dilts—October—Lab Report
Objective: To get Grant to notice me.

Materials: Variety of health and beauty aids
as supplied by Dixie Finch.
Methods: Surrender to the capable hands of
Dixie Finch.

Distance wise, Dixie's house is not too far from where I live. He lives at 2161 Richmond Street, which is just on the other side of school, not far from the interstate. His neighborhood is distinctly different from the one my family lives in. The streets are narrower and almost all of the houses are the same one-story ranch style. Dixie's house is only a block from the strip mall where his mom works. It's painted a dark yellow with black shutters and sits on a very small patch of land equal in size to every other lot on the street. I walk up the very short path to the door and ring the bell.

Dixie opens the door and says, "Ah, madame. You are here for your beauty makeover, no?" He is trying to use a French accent, but it clashes with his natural southern twang, so the words sound funny. I almost laugh but remember that Dixie gets laughed at enough at school, so I make sure to stifle my giggles. Dixie drops his French accent and welcomes me in. "Oh, dearie, I could barely sleep last night thinking about the transformation we are going to create today. That Grant Bradish is going to sit up and take notice like Maurice Chevalier did with Leslie Caron in *Gigi*."

Once again I have no idea what movie he is referring to, but at least I am getting used to his cinematic references. Dixie looks down and sees the wheeled suitcase I brought with me.

"Good," he say, "you brought luggage. You are here for the long haul. I like a girl who can really make a commitment to her beauty regime."

"Actually, I have to be home for dinner. My mom is trying out a new recipe." I wheel the suitcase through the doorway. "This contains most of the outfits I bought before school started when I thought fashion alone would make me popular. Most of them still have the tags on them. I thought you might be able to see if any of it is salvageable."

"Fabulous," Dixie says, and takes the suitcase farther into the house. Dixie's house is small but charming. As soon as you enter, you are in the living room and you can see the kitchen/dining room area from the doorway. I look the other way down the short hall and see a few doors to what

I assume are the bedrooms and bathroom. "C'mon," Dixie says, and grabs my hand. "I have everything set up in the kitchen. That's where my mother does a lot of her practice work for the salon."

The kitchen looks like any normal kitchen at first glance, but if you study it for a moment you begin to realize a few of the details are off. There is a blow-dryer where a blender should be, and while most kitchens have a jar containing spatulas and wooden spoons, this one has a jar with hair-brushes and a curling iron. Dixie opens one of the cabinets and instead of cereal or mixing bowls, there are rows of hair sprays, moisturizers, nail polishes, and a few items in colorful, sleek containers that I don't even recognize.

"Oh my God!" I say.

"Are you freaked out a bit?" Dixie asks. I think this may be the first time he has revealed this particular family secret.

"Not at all," I say with complete sincerity. "I mean, I have never seen a kitchen like this before but it's incredible."

"My mom hardly ever cooks, so it just makes sense to use the kitchen for a more practical purpose." Dixie shrugs his shoulders and smiles. I can see he is more relaxed now that he has shown me his laboratory. In a way Dixie is a scientist too. While my lab has microscopes and spread-sheets, his has hair dye and nail files. Really it's just the other side of the same coin.

"Let's get started. I spent last night and this morning going through the major fashion and beauty magazines that my mom gets for the salon and ripped out the pictures of the looks I think will most attract Grant based on a general style composite of the Holly Trinity and what looks are hot right now. To be honest with you, some of what the Holly Trinity wears is so twenty minutes ago. I mean, seriously, it would not kill those girls to pick up a copy of *Paris Vogue* every now and then. What do you think about this?" Dixie asks, and hands me a picture from a magazine. "Or this? Or this one without the bangs from hell?"

We spend the next hour talking and laughing over the pictures while Dixie mixes together the ingredients for our series of extreme facials. He figures he could use one too. First he cracks open a few eggs and carefully separates the yolk from the white. He throws out the yolk and mixes the whites with a few more ingredients and then finds a wide brush on the counter and paints my face with the mixture. "This will help tighten your pores."

As soon as he makes the first stroke I say out loud,

"Albumen." Why didn't I think of this earlier? This is so obvious. I'm almost embarrassed.

"Huh?" Dixie says as he continues to brush.

"Albumen is the protein contained in egg whites. It constricts as it dries so of course it makes the perfect facial ingredient." As I say the last few words I can feel the egg whites drying and tightening around my face. The sensation is unusual if not entirely unpleasant.

After this procedure, Dixie prepares an oatmeal moisturizer and a cucumber eye cooler. As we are lying on the living room floor with oatmeal on our faces and cucumbers slices over our eyes, the front door opens.

"Hi, kids. Don't get up, y'all. I know how important it is to not interrupt a beauty treatment." Dixie's mom walks between us and toward the hall.

"Hi, Mom," Dixie says from underneath the oatmeal. I'm not sure what to say. I've never met someone for the first time while lying on her living room floor covered in produce.

"Hi, Mrs. Finch. I'm Dorie," I say.

"Yes, Tommy, I mean Dixie, has told me all about you. How is your experiment going?" she asks.

"Good. Dixie has been a tremendous help."

"Well, I'll be in the bedroom if you two need me." Mrs.

Finch steps over my body and then over Tommy's, and heads out of the room. Dixie and I wash our faces in the kitchen sink, but when I use the word "wash" Dixie fakes having a heart attack.

"Dorie, dearie, you wash the dishes. We *cleanse* our skin." He says the word "cleanse" slowly and deliberately.

Now that he has completed what he calls nourishing and enriching my complexion, he says it is time to begin some facial shaping.

"What exactly is facial shaping?" I ask.

"Well, in your case it means dealing with your eyebrows or, dare I say, eyebrow." He winces a bit as he says it, hoping he will not offend me. I pick up one of the hand mirrors on the counter and look at the space above my eyes. I've never really examined it before, but there does seem to be a lack of definition from the ending of one brow to the beginning of the next. Behind me I see Dixie holding a slim pair of tweezers. "Oh, no," I say.

"Now, Dorie, this won't hurt that much." He goes to the freezer and takes out an ice cube. "First I am going to numb the area with an ice cube."

"Dixie, if this isn't going to hurt then why do you need to numb anything?"

Dixie doesn't answer me. He puts the cold ice cube on my eyebrows, pats my face dry with a towel, and then plucks out the very first hair.

"Ow!" I scream.

"I know, dearie. Try not to focus on the pain. Think about the result." In my head I try to visualize my lab notebook, and I can almost see the word "objective" followed by "to be popular." I use this as my mantra as Dixie plucks out each rebellious piece of eye brow hair. With each pluck I can actually feel myself getting closer and closer to my objective.

A few hours later I have been plucked, polished, and perfumed. Dixie has created what he calls a few fabulous "looks" putting together some of the clothes I brought over in combinations I would never have dreamed of. Mrs. Finch actually showed me how to blow-dry my hair so that the end curl looks bouncy and casual, not rigid and plastic.

At the end of the afternoon Dixie finally says, "All right, darlin', it's time for the reveal." He moves some coats that are hanging on hooks in front of the closet door to expose a full-length mirror. Dixie guides me by the hand to a spot in front of the mirror and instructs me to keep my eyes closed. I am unprepared to observe even the slightest change in my appearance. Part of me wants to keep my eyes closed and run to the nearest shower and let the water wash any change away, but then Dixie says, "Open your eyes."

I slowly release my eyelids from their tight grip and open my eyes. "Wow," I say. I don't look like a totally different person like on some makeover show. I still look like myself, but I feel like I look like *my best self.* "Thank you so much," I say.

"Do you like it?" Dixie asks. "I know it's not as dramatic as Melanie Griffith in *Working Girl,* but I figured we would at least take some baby steps."

"I love it. I feel beautiful."

"Dorie, you *are* beautiful. Grant Bradish is definitely going to notice you now."

CHAPTER

"Let the experiment be made."

—Benjamin Franklin

Monday morning I am ready to put the next stage of my experiment into action. Before I take a shower and prepare myself, I look over my lab notebook to remind myself of each step I need to take in order to accomplish my goal. Before I left Dixie's house I actually let him write down the steps of my new beauty regime in my lab notebook. I have never in my life allowed anyone else to read my lab notebook let alone write something down in it. However, Dixie has done so much to help me that I figured he earned a place in the documentation. After all, if this works, I might consider selling my notebooks online so that other girls of above-average scientific intelligence can take advantage of my social experiment.

Since Dixie has used a purple glitter gel pen for his section, some of the writing is blurred, but I can still read most of it. He has given me small sample sizes of each of the products he believes I should use. There is a special moisturizer for combination skin, shampoo to lock in moisture, and some moisture-enriched makeup. I may not know a lot about beauty treatments, but one thing I have learned is that it is a lot like good cake: the moister the better.

Dixie has agreed to meet me outside the back door of the school's west wing right before my Scientific Inquiries class. He will see if I need any touch-ups. I race down the stairs after my English class and sprint down the hall to meet Dixie. I throw open the doors, and Dixie is standing there holding a large makeup brush already dipped in a very soft pink blush. "I knew we would need to freshen the blush first," he says. "Close your eyes and use this hair brush to smooth out some of the flyaways in the back of your hair." I do as I'm told and in the time it takes to change classes at Greenview, Dixie and I have completely refreshed my look.

I walk into Scientific Inquiries, and Mr. Evans is thankfully working on putting up some announcement on the computer wipe board at the front of the room. Instead of taking my usual front row position I try to saunter my way to the back of the classroom and take a seat near Grant. I open up my bag and pretend to look for a pencil. Then I say, "Oh, no. I seem to have forgotten my pencil." I take one hand and move it to the back of my neck and flip my hair over my shoulder. I practiced this move so many times this weekend I thought I was developing a rash. I turn toward Grant, who has his back to me, and say, "Excuse me, do you happen to have a pencil I could borrow?"

Grant does not turn around. I am not sure what to do. I flip my hair once more and say more loudly, "Excuse me, do you happen to have a pencil I could borrow?" This time I hold out my hand hoping he will turn around, see how good I look, and be compelled to drop a writing implement into my waiting palm.

Grant finally begins to turn around but just as he does Sumita Patel, who is seated directly behind me, says, "Dorie, I have plenty. Take two of mine," and drops two mechanical pencils in my palm. Before I am able to remove them Grant has turned completely around to face me. He looks at me and then he looks down at the two pencils suddenly in my palm. Then he looks me in the face again. I can't tell if he is noticing my new appearance or if he is confirming his suspicion that I am certifiably mentally insane.

Before I am able to decide, Mr. Evans begins class. "All right, everyone. We have a lot to do today and I need to save some time at the end of class to make a special announcement, so let's get started. Please open your textbooks to the beginning of chapter four. Could I have a volunteer to read through the first equation on the page?"

Someone near the front of the room raises his hand, and I pretend to be very interested in the equation so that I can bury my head in the book. I try to ignore the fact that Grant might still be staring at me, wondering about my level of sanity. I spend the rest of the period furiously taking notes and responding to Mr. Evans' questions so that Grant will see that while I may have the social skills of a wild boar, I do at least have some level of intelligence.

Near the end of class Mr. Evans asks us to close our books and give our attention to the giant flat-screen monitor behind him. He says, "This may take a moment. I am still getting used to all of this technology in the new lab. Some days I miss my old chalkboard. Ah, here it is." Mr.

Evans clicks a button and the screen switches on. The announcement reads: "To inaugurate the new labs generously donated by Bradish Pharmaceutical, Greenview Middle School will present . . ." The black letters on the screen fade out, and large block letters in the school's colors quickly fade in. "TWENTY-EIGHT GREAT EXPERIMENTS THAT CHANGED THE WORLD." Everyone in the class starts whispering. No one knows exactly what this all means, but the presentation was certainly dramatic enough to warrant a certain level of buzz.

"We will spend our class time studying twenty-eight great scientific experiments that changed the world, and you will each present a version of that experiment as your project." Mr. Evans gathers some papers from his desk and begins to distribute them to the class. "This page contains a list of the experiments that we will be considering. Each Friday one team will present their experiment. I will give you plenty of time to choose the experiment you would like to work on, but first I will need you to choose your lab partners. Anyone who does not self-select, will be assigned a partner."

Great. Well, I've been down this road before. No one ever chooses me as a partner. I'll just have to wait until everyone else decides who they are working with and see who is left. I continue to twirl the ends of my hair not caring if it straightens the curl.

"So, who knows with whom they would like to work?" Mr. Evans asks. Of course, Grant's hand shoots straight up. He and Doug are permanently joined at the hip. I'm surprised he has to even announce his choice of partner, but one can always count on Grant to state the obvious. Mr. Evans calls on Grant.

"I choose her," Grant says, and points in my general direction.

"Me?" Carrie Rodgers screams as if she has won the lottery. Carrie is very pretty, so I can understand why Grant might forsake Doug for her.

"No," Grant says loudly. "Not her. The other one. That Darlene girl." There is no Darlene in class. Now he is the one who seems a bit insane. Who could he be talking about?

"Do you mean Dorie?" Mr. Evans asks. Ha. Ha. Thanks a lot Mr. Evans. Make a joke at my expense.

"Yeah, yeah," Grant says. "I want Doris as my partner. This girl with the straight hair on one side and curly hair on the other." I immediately take my hand away from my hair and stop playing with it. Oh my God. He is talking about me.

"Her name is Dorie, not Doris," Mr. Evans says. "Are you interested in being Grant's partner, Doris? I mean, Dorie."

I don't know what to say. Being Grant's partner would be a perfect way to get involved with and dumped by Grant. This would surely help my experiment to be in with the Holly Trinity. I'm simply stunned by the whole turn of events. I can't really speak so I nod my head vigorously up and down. Mr. Evans marks it down in his notebook. As he writes down the other partners, I think about how I am going to thank Dixie for all his help. I can't believe it actually worked. The right outfit and the right styling made all of the difference. I went from being someone totally invisible to Grant to someone that he wants to spend the rest of the marking period working with.

When the bell rings, I slowly put my books in my bag so that I will exit the room at the same time Grant does. As I see him approach the door, I sling my backpack over my shoulder and head toward him. Unfortunately, we both hit the narrow entrance at the same exact time and get stuck together for a second.

"Oh my God. I'm sorry," I say, and let him pass before me.

"Don't sweat it, Doris."

"Actually, it's Dorie."

"What's Dorie?" he asks.

"I am," I say. "That's my name."

"Yeah, right, Dorie."

"Look," I say, "it's great that you picked me as your partner. It will really give us a chance to get to know each
other better." I flip my hair in that special way I have been
practicing but most of it falls in front of my eyes so I have
to brush it out of the way with my hand. By the time I
have done that, though, Grant has already moved down the
hall toward his locker. He stops at his locker and sees that
I am still behind him.

"Hey, Dorie . . ." He got my name right. Hooray. This is
definitely moving in the right direction. "Don't get
excited. I always pick the smartest kid in class to be my
partner." Then he looks me up and down and adds, "Even
if it is a girl."

My jaw literally drops open. Who in the world does this
conceited jerk think he is? I am shocked that he would
admit to such underhanded ulterior motives. Not to
mention his completely sexist comment. *Even if it is a
girl?* Someone get this boy a calendar. My God, it's the
twenty-first century. Like girls have any less intelligence.
I bet if this were an assignment for English class or home

economics, he wouldn't have any problem choosing a girl. I'm furious. I can feel the blood in my veins boiling. I open my mouth to scream at him. "You listen here, Grant . . ."

I can only get the first few words out of my mouth before someone pokes Grant in the shoulder. "What you doing, Bradish? Working on your next conquest?" I turn to see who is talking to Grant, and it is the *entire* Holly Trinity. As soon as they make their comment they seemingly erupt in a fit of laughter and continue walking down the hall. Grant slams his fist against the locker in anger, and I watch the Trinity continue down the hall. I never cease to be amazed at how close they are. There is nothing one of them does that the other two do not support. I feel that pang in my stomach, that longing to be part of their group, that strong desire to be popular at all costs.

Grant suddenly remembers I was talking to him before the Holly Trinity drive-by. "So, what were you saying?"

Phew. If the Holly Trinity had not come by when they did, I might have ruined the whole thing. I take a deep breath to remind myself to stay on target. You can do this, Dorie.

"I was just wondering when you wanted to get together to work on the project," I say.

CHAPTER

13

"The best scientist is open to experience and begins with romance—the idea that anything is possible." —Ray Bradbury

As soon as I get home I head straight up to my room and put a very satisfying check mark next to the first item on my procedure list: Get Grant to learn my name. I can't believe I've been able to get so far with my experiment so quickly. It just goes to show you that when you have the right list of materials and a good set of procedures you can accomplish anything. I turn to the calendar in the front of my notebook. This is the second week of October. That should be plenty of time to get dumped by Grant and be

P. G. Kain

counseled, comforted, and accepted by the the Holly Trinity before the end of the year.

I lean back on my bed and close my eyes. I don't necessarily believe in positive visualization, but I figure it can't hurt. I picture arriving at Greenview the day of my next birthday. I walk down the hall toward homeroom and for a moment I think it's just another birthday. Then I turn the corner to put my coat in my locker and there it is. Pink crepe paper, purple balloons, white flowers made out of tissue paper. My locker looks like it has been entered in the Macy's Thanksgiving Day Parade. I walk closer to my locker and there on the front door is a sign with big block letters drawn with sparkly gel pen: HAPPY BIRTHDAY, DORIE! LUV, HOLLY, JENNY, AND ALEXIS. I know it is entirely silly and a decorated locker is just a superficial thing, but I want it. I really want it. I want people to see my locker and think, *That Dorie girl has some really cool friends who went to a lot of trouble to decorate her locker.* It's like a scientific equation. everyone has heard $E=MC^2$. On paper that E is meaningless. It's just a letter. But when you find out the E stands for energy, you realize it isn't just a letter at all. It means something. It means something important. I'm not equating Einstein to a crepe-paper garland, but—

"Dorie!" my Mom yells from the kitchen. "You have a telephone call." I must have been so wrapped up in my daydream that I totally missed the phone ringing. Oh my God. What if it's Grant? What if he has already reviewed the list of Twenty-Eight Great Experiments and selected his favorites before I've even had a chance to review everything? What if he has picked an experiment that is too simple to replicate? I race down to the kitchen and grab the phone from my mom and run to the family room almost out of breath.

"Hello," I say.

"Dorie, are you all right?"

"Oh, it's you. I thought it might be Grant," I say nonchalantly. Perhaps it is cruel to overexcite Dixie this way, but I cannot resist the temptation.

"OHMYGAWD! OHMYGAWD! It worked. It worked." I can hear Dixie hollering and cheering. I can't tell exactly, but it sounds like he has dropped the phone on the floor and is dancing around his living room. I don't think I've had anyone be so excited for me in my entire life.

"Dixie! Dixie!" I shout into the phone to try to get his attention.

"I knew it. I knew it. I wasn't going to give your hair

that last set of deep conditioners, but I said to myself, 'Dixie, you go all out on Miss Dorie's head. You give her hair the luster and body it needs to get Grant's attention and it worked. I—'"

"Dixie." I try to stop him before he begins an encore performance. I don't have the heart to tell him that the makeover may be only partially responsible for the recent turn of events.

"So tell me. I want to hear everything, and if you leave out one detail I will not give you my secret recipe for the cucumber oatmeal facial." I do as Dixie asks and tell him everything that happened. If I even try to gloss over even the smallest detail Dixie stops me and makes me go back and flush out whatever I skipped.

"Dorie Dilts and Grant Bradish lab partners. I can't believe it," Dixie says once I have finished the story. "I think it's very Bogie and Bacall."

Finally, a movie reference I get. "You mean Humphrey Bogart and Lauren Bacall," I say casually.

"Well done, my dear." Dixie is impressed that I finally caught one of his references. "I'm sure you know then that they were one of Hollywood's most unlikely couples. Perhaps you and Grant will also find a true romantic connection. Imagine." Dixie begins to use a dreamy singsong tone. "The two of you staring at amoebas together through a microscope in a lab lit only by the soft glow of Bunsen burners. Cut to a close-up of him. Cut to a close-up of her."

"Fade out," I say, and cut him off. Dixie is getting carried away with himself. "This is not about anything romantic. This is about becoming popular. Remember, getting involved with Grant is just a means to an end. The ultimate goal is to get him to dump me."

"But . . ."

"No 'buts,' Dixie. A good scientist does not lose track of her goals and desired outcomes."

"But . . ."

"A good scientist reviews her strategies and maintains a sharp focus."

Dixie finally surrenders. "Oh, all right. I'm just saying that if things work out for you and Grant, maybe—"

Dixie is interrupted when my mother calls my name from the kitchen.

"Dorie! Come set the table for dinner, please!"

"I have to go set the table, Dix."

"Okay. Just make sure I know when you guys decide to have your first study session."

"Of course," I say.

"And, remember, Dorie, *details*, I relish *details*." I laugh out loud when Dixie says this. He really knows how to crack me up. I hang up with Dixie and head to the kitchen to help my mom. She is in the middle of concocting a Moroccan couscous that demands her full focus, so I grab the plates and silverware, and start setting the table without disturbing her.

As I set the table, I can't help thinking about what Dixie said on the phone. Sure, Grant is one of the cutest guys at school. I guess I just have never really thought about the possibility of liking *liking* Grant since I have never really thought about boys in that way. Not seriously at least. I guess I've had some crushes on some guys, but those were mostly from a safe distance—like in fourth grade when we had this substitute, Mr. Crow, who I thought had the softest blue eyes I had ever seen. I would pray at night that our regular teacher would get sick and Mr. Crow would be our permanent sub. I also wanted to write fan letters to Anderson Cooper after I started watching the evening news with my dad. Those were just crushes, nothing serious.

It always seemed to me that boyfriends came and went. Back in Rancho I watched Amanda Donohue date four different guys in less than a school year, but she had been best friends with Julie Tavner since the third grade. Grant dated and dumped every girl in the Holly Trinity. Now he doesn't even acknowledge any of them in the hall while Holly, Jenny, and Alexis are tighter than particles in an atom. When you are in with the popular girls, you have something you can depend on, something that will last. Really, when it comes down to it, it's a simple matter of numbers. I'd rather have years of friendship than a few months of romance. You don't need a spreadsheet to figure that out.

CHAPTER

14

"They are ill discoverers that think there is
no land, when they can see nothing but sea."
—Francis Bacon

After four e-mails, three telephone messages, and countless instant messages spanning Friday afternoon through Sunday evening, I finally decide to give up after making one last telephone call. I dial the number, which I memorized shortly after looking it up in the phone book the other day. I've already left three messages, so if I don't actually speak to a real person, I'll just hang up. The phone rings and after the third ring someone picks up.

"Hello," an adult female voice says with polished calm. I assume this is Grant's mother.

"Hello, Mrs. Bradish? I'm trying to reach Grant." My voice trembles with uncertainty. I'm still working on developing my "phone voice."

"Alexis, is that you? How have you been, sweetie? I'm sorry Grant's not here—"

"Um, ah, no." I try to interrupt Mrs. Bradish, but she just keeps talking. Then she says the name again. *Alexis.* She thinks I'm Alexis, Grant's most recent girlfriend and designated dumpee. Ohmygod. I know this is only a case of mistaken identity but the coincidence thrills me. To believe that someone would actually mistake me for a member of the Holly Trinity (even if only an adult, and on the phone at that, but still). This is definitely a small triumph. This must mean on some level that my experiment is moving along in the right direction. I almost don't correct Mrs. Bradish. Part of me wants to let her go on thinking I'm Alexis, but I realize that the success of our science projects depends of getting in contact with Grant before school on Monday.

"Actually, I'm Dorie," I say. "Dorie Dilts. I'm Grant's new lab partner."

Her tone changes significantly. "Oh, I see. Well, I'll tell him you called." She is all business. Even adults recognize the power of popularity.

"Thank you," I say. "It's very important I get in touch with him." She assures me she will give him the message.

Monday morning I get to school early hoping I will see Grant by his locker. Today is the day Mr. Evans is going to let us select the experiment we are going to work on. The halls are empty, and I pace up and down worried that Grant has his mind set on an experiment that I know won't work. I've prepared a list of my top three choices and also made note of a few of the experiments that I absolutely know will be duds. Sure, the invention of barometric pressure changed the way we forecast weather, but how impressive is it to pluck a stray hair and watch it expand and contract in correspondence with the humidity in the room? Big deal. If Grant is determined to work on barometric pressure I don't know what I'll do. I'll just show him my top three choices and explain why each of those would make a better choice.

Suddenly I see Grant surrounded by a group of guys. "Grant. Grant!" I shout across the hall. This is my last chance to confer with him before Mr. Evans makes us submit our first three choices. Grant sees me and breaks away from the group of guys.

"Geesh. Did somebody die or something?"

"What are you talking about?" I sure hope no one has died.

"All the messages and e-mails and stuff. What do you want?" Is he putting me on? Surely he knows that our selections are due today.

"Twenty-Eight Great Experiments?" I say. "Our selection is due today."

"Oh that. Yeah. I've been thinking about that—" I don't let him finish. He's sandbagging me. He's trying to make me think he doesn't care and then casually suggest we do barometric pressure. Well, think again, Bradish. I'm not that easy to fool.

"Look, so have I," I say, barely giving him a chance to speak. "I think the top three choices have to be—"

"Okay. Fine. See you in class." He cuts me off before I even announce a single experiment.

"What? You haven't even heard my choices."

"I was just gonna pick the first one on the list, but if you're in love with one of the other ones, I don't care. That's fine. Whatever. Look, I gotta go. Just sign up in class."

Grant walks away and I am just standing there. I don't know if this is good news or bad news. I'm glad I get to choose, but one would have thought he would have had a little more enthusiasm for the project. I decide not to dwell on the downside and take comfort in the fact that we will not be working on the discovery of barometric pressure.

I try to nail things down with Grant again before class, but he strolls in with his sidekick Doug just as the bell rings. As Mr. Evans prepares the materials for class I go over my list of top choices. My first choice is George Ohm and the discovery of Ohm's Law. I pray no one else picks this since I have some great ideas about how to recreate Ohm's famous experiment. My second choice is Edison and the invention of the light bulb, but that is such an obvious crowd-pleaser that I think there is little chance that one will get assigned without a fight for it. Also creating the vacuum seal for the filament is much harder than it looks. My third choice is Robert Millikan's Oil-Drop Experiment, which determined the charge of an electron. You need an X-ray machine to do this one, but I bet we could borrow one from my dad's lab.

Mr. Evans starts class and I try to stay focused on my list. "As you know, students, today is the day we will be making selections for Twenty-Eight Great Experiments. I think the easiest way to do this is to go down the list alphabetically." That may be the easiest, but it sure isn't the fairest. My last name begins with a *D*. By the time he gets to me all of the good ones will be gone. Then I remember that Grant is my lab partner, and his last name begins with a *B*. The only person I have to worry about is Donna Abitabilo.

I turn around to see if I can get Grant's attention, but he is whispering something to Doug and not looking anywhere near my direction. Since Ohm's Law deals with voltage I hold up two fingers in the *V*-for-victory shape and hope Grant will look over at me. Surely, he will get the hint.

"I'm working with Uli Yablonski, and we would like to do Foucault's Pendulum," Donna says. Uli really lucked out getting a partner with such an alphabetically fortunate last name. I realize Mr. Evans will call on Grant next. I have my body almost completely turned around in my seat and I'm shaking my hand so hard I think it might fall off but still Grant does not see me.

"Grant Bradish," Mr. Evans calls, "what have you selected?" Grant looks down at his desk and just stares at the handout with the list of experiments. What is wrong with him? I am trying to communicate with him telekinetically but my best efforts are being wasted. Grant does not even glance in my direction. I just pray that he will have enough sense to see that Ohm's Law is truly the best experiment to recreate. Grant keeps staring at the list and does not respond to Mr. Evans. I hold out my fingers in the *V* formation again straining my hand as if the extra effort will make a difference.

"Mr. Bradish, what have you selected?"

"I dunno. How about this Macaroni guy?"

The class almost begins to laugh but only a few stray giggles escape. No one dare laugh at the coolest kid in school even if his mistake is rather hysterical.

"Do you mean Marconi and the invention of the wireless radio?" Mr. Evans asks.

"Yeah, that one," Grant says without missing a beat. It is amazing how he can make such a stupid mistake and not feel embarrassed at all. If I had done something like that I'd be running to the girls' room on the verge of tears, but Grant just shakes it off like he intended to make the mistake.

"Good luck, Mr. Bradish. The wireless radio is quite a challenge," Mr. Evans says, and then moves on to the next person on the list.

Quite a challenge? Please. I was making transistor radios with my dad in fourth grade. How much harder can a wireless radio be? I should be able to do this one in my sleep. I look over at Grant who has already tuned class out. For a second I consider going up to Mr. Evans after class and asking him if I can change lab partners. Then I remember if I am looking for a scientific challenge this marking period I already have it. Maybe in thirty years from now some science teacher in some classroom of the future will assign Twenty-Nine Great Experiments, and some kids will fight over the chance to re-create the social experiments of Dorie Dilts. Of course for that to happen I need to make sure I stay focused on the project at hand. As Mr. Evans makes his way down the list I pull out my lab notebook to chart my progress.

"When science finally locates the center of the universe, some people will be surprised to learn they're not it." —Bernard Bailey

Back in Rancho the difference between summer and winter was negligible. In fact some technically summer days were much colder than any winter day. The landscape was almost completely unaltered by the change in seasons. A yucca plant is a yucca plant is a yucca plant. In New Jersey autumn emotionally begins in mid-October. The mornings start getting colder and everything changes from monochromatic green to a brew of yellows, reds, and oranges.

As I walk to school, I can't help but stare at the trees that line the street. Some of the bigger ones must be more than a hundred years old and their leaves are spectacular. Each one has a different hue. It looks like each leaf was hand painted. Of course, I realize that the changing leaf color is simply a matter of sunlight turning water and carbon dioxide into glucose. But I can't stop staring at the trees.

As I approach school I notice there is some type of hubbub happening on the steps. I wonder if it is some kind of official school event I somehow forgot to take notice of. As I get closer I notice Holly is at the top of the stairs. She looks beautiful. She is wearing an army green halter-top dress with orange and blue flowers embroidered from the waist down to the hem. She is smiling that one-hundred-watt smile of hers and acting a little embarrassed. Alexis and Jenny are fussing about her. I move closer to see what exactly is going on.

"Holly, you know the tradition. The birthday girl wears the crown," Jenny says, and hands Holly a rhinestone tiara like you might see in a teen beauty pageant.

"Oh, all right," Holly says, placing the tiara on the top of her head.

"All hail, Holly McAdams, birthday princess!" Alexis shouts. A small crowd has gathered around them and joins

Alexis in her cheer. The entire Holly Trinity is giggling and Holly sits at the top of the steps as Alexis and Jenny each pick up a huge flat box and start moving through the crowd. Suddenly, I'm face to face with Jenny. She holds her box in front of me, and I can now see it is filled with cupcakes frosted with white icing and baby blue *H*'s for Holly, obviously.

"Would you like a cupcake? We're celebrating Holly's birthday," Jenny says.

This is the first time she has spoken directly to me. For a second I don't say anything. I imagine this time next year hanging out with Holly, Jenny, and Alexis, and reminiscing about the first time we actually met. "Remember," I'll say, "we met when you offered me a cupcake for Holly's birthday last year."

"Oh, yeah," she'll say, and then we will laugh about how long ago that seems and how it seems like we have always been friends, the four of us, and how—

"HEY!" The voice snaps me out of the daydream. "Do you want a cupcake or not? This isn't the school cafeteria. We're trying to do something nice for you people on Holly's birthday."

This *is* incredibly nice of them. "Yeah, I'd love one," I say, and grab the one closest to me. "These look great. I love cupcakes." I quickly unwrap the confection and put way too much of it in my mouth. However, this does not stop me from waxing poetic about the treat. "Yum-o. These are so moist. Wow, are these moist or what? You have just the right frosting to cake ratio. Well done."

Jenny just stares at me. I know I should stop talking. I should just say "Thank you." Two simple words and that should be the end of it, but I can't help it. I just keep talking and talking like my mouth is missing an off switch. The fact that my face is covered in frosting and crumbs doesn't really impede my talking, I just go on and on. "You guys really know how to make a good cupcake. You should think about selling these. They are that good. I mean it. They are really good."

"You know," Jenny finally interrupts me, "you shouldn't talk with your mouth full."

"I know. How rude of me," I say, but Jenny does not wait for my response. She just walks away as I continue to talk *at her*. "Sorry about that. Well thanks for the cupcake." At this point she is a significant distance away from me so I shout the last part. "SEE YOU LATER!" A small explosion of crumbs pops out of my mouth. A few of the kids around me stop and stare. Since Jenny is so far away, it's not clear exactly to whom I am speaking.

The school bell rings and all the kids rush into the building. I move to the side of the steps to let everyone pass.

So my interaction with the Trinity wasn't exactly ideal, but at least I had some type of interaction. I've moved from completely invisible to a minor nuisance. That has got to be an improvement.

As I lick some of the lingering stickiness off my fingers a huge maple tree with fiery red leaves that were once grass green catches my eye. This huge tree that I had only seen green and verdant is now completely different. I take a deep breath in and realize how grateful I am to be living in a place with seasonal variety. It makes me feel like anything is possible.

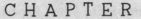

CHAPTER

"Science shows us what exists but not what to do about it." —Heinz R. Pagels

M om, it's not a study date. Would you please stop calling it that?"

"I'm sorry, dear. I should have said would you like me to make some snacks for your study *session*," my mom says, correcting her mistake. Just because a boy is coming over to the house to study my mom automatically assumes it's a study date.

"Actually, we are kind of behind on this project, and I don't think we are going to have any time for snacks."

"That's unlike you, to be behind on your schoolwork," my mom says as she walks across the kitchen to sit next to me at the dining room table where I have all of the materials for the Twenty-Eight Great Experiments project laid out. "Is everything going all right at school? I know moving to a new school can be a very traumatic experience for a young person, but you seem to be adjusting just fine."

I really dislike being called a *young person*. It's an absolutely juvenile expression. My little brother is a young person. I see no reason why I just can't be called a teen. However, instead of getting on my soapbox about this with my mother I just let her know that my schoolwork is fine and that I am doing a very good job of adjusting. Of course, I'll be doing a much better job once I get Grant to dump me, but I keep that part to myself.

"The only real problem is getting my new lab partner, Grant, to commit to some time to work on our project. We haven't even decided on the list of procedures or anything, and whenever Mr. Evans gives us time to work in class Grant finds a way to spend the time talking to his pal Doug about basketball or snowboarding or some other nonscientific pursuit."

"Well, maybe you should talk to Mr. Evans. Maybe he will assign you a new partner."

"No!" I shout quickly and a little too loudly. I've spent

the entire school year so far working on my social experiment. I'm not about to give up now. Getting Grant as my
lab partner has been the luckiest break I've had.

The doorbell rings and I get up to answer it. Grant is
twenty minutes late. By the time I get to the door the car
that dropped Grant off is already speeding away.

"You're like almost a half hour late Grant," I say. I'm not
trying to scold him. I'm simply pointing out a fact.

"Yeah, I know. You think I don't know how to tell time?
I had to wait for my brother to get back from the hospital
to drive me over."

"Oh, is he all right? Was he in an accident?"

"He's fine. He is a resident over at Somerset Medical.
He's gonna be a doctor."

"Wow. He must be really smart."

I have obviously hit a sore spot with Grant. He rolls his
eyes and storms past me. "Yeah, yeah," he says. "I've heard
it all before—how he got all the brains—so spare me."

"Let's work in the dining room," I say. "There's a big
table in there and a lot of good light."

Grant walks through the vestibule and into the dining
room. For a second I'm distracted by the way he walks. He
moves through space like he's listening to his own private

soundtrack. All the other boys at school are so awkward and unsure. They all shuffle their feet like part of their heel is permanently attached to the floor. No wonder so many of the guys at school look up to him and want to be his friend.

Grant takes a seat at the dining room table and throws his backpack on the table creating a breeze that blows most of my notes on to the floor.

"What's the big idea?" I shout, running over to the other end of the table and gathering my papers from the floor. "Do you have any idea how long it has taken me to organize all of this information?" Luckily I have already color coded most of the research with individual Post-it notes so putting it back together won't be that much work, but Grant doesn't know that.

"Sorry," he says, but I can tell he doesn't mean it. "You got anything to eat?"

"Are you serious? We have sooo much to—"

Just then my mother enters the dining room carrying a tray.

"Hi, kids. I know you didn't think you would want a snack, but I had some leftover minitacos from the other night that I thought I would just heat up. If you want them, great. If not, that's no problem," my mom says, putting the tray on the far end of the table away from my notes. "You must be Grant. Nice to meet you."

"Hello, Mrs. Dilts." Grant actually stands up when he greets my mother. I'm surprised at his good manners. I would have thought he would have shoved a taco in his mouth before he even acknowledged her. My mother is clearly impressed by his manners. Parents are always impressed by good manners, and I'm sure Grant knows this and works it for all it's worth.

My mother asks Grant a few parental-unit type questions and then leaves us alone to work. The minute she leaves the room Grant attacks the tray of food. "These look awesome. Is your mom like a professional chef? That's so cool. I've been thinking about doing that."

"Grant!" I shout, moving my books and papers away from him. "You are getting salsa on my book from the library."

"Sorry," he says, and again I can tell he doesn't mean it.

"Look, we need to get started on this project. It's due in a few weeks and even though we are really behind, I think we can get everything done if we stick to a schedule. Now, before we start working on the experiment itself, we need to do the preliminary historical research and develop a presentation." I hand Grant the assignment sheet Mr. Evans gave out in class. "I've circled the grade percentage he assigned for each part of the project and as you can see Mr. Evans has placed a lot of evidence on historical research, which I can understand because a good scientist needs to know—"

"Yeah. Yeah," Grant says, and starts looking out the dining room toward the other end of the house. "Where's your TV? The snowboard finals are in a few minutes. You guys get satellite, right?"

"Grant, have you been listening to a word I've said?"

He grabs another mini taco and puts it in his mouth. "Not really. Anyway, do you guys get SAT TV or what?"

"Grant, we have got to start putting some serious work into this project. I realize building a radio is not the most complex of the projects." I try to hide my anger and disappointment about this reality. "Still, we need to start working on the research or else we will never even get a chance to start working on the lab report."

Grant gets up from his chair. Finally, he must be coming to his senses. I think he is going to pick up one of the books from the other end of the table, but instead of doing that he just keeps walking out of the room.

"Where are you going?" I shout after him.

"Mike Wong lives like a few houses down the road."

"So?" I ask.

"So," he says as if I am an idiot, "he has satellite and a huge hi-def plasma TV." He grabs his backpack off the table. "I'm headed over there to watch the finals. Thank your mom for the snacks. They were awesome. See you later, Dorie."

Grant walks to the door. He smiles at me and waves before he lets the door fall closed behind him.

I can feel the blood boil in my veins.

CHAPTER

"We are continually faced with a series of great opportunities brilliantly disguised as insoluble problems." —John W. Gardner

The next day I stop in on Dixie in the library during my lunch period to catch him up on all the gory details. I've never been the type of person to really reveal too much about my personal life to someone else. Part of me has simply always considered my private life, well, private. Another part of me realizes the reason I haven't really shared too much of my life with other people is that no one outside my family has really been that interested. Dixie, however, seems endlessly interested in every detail of my experiment. He loves to help me brainstorm new ideas and refine my procedures. At first I thought he was as interested in the science part of the experiment as I am, but lately I think he just likes talking with someone who values his opinion so much.

"Hey, Dixie," I say as I pass through the turnstiles.

"Hey, darlin'," he says, smiling. "Did you bring your lunch? Don't worry, nobody else is here."

I feel funny bringing my lunch to eat in the library. Dixie is allowed to eat here because he actually works in the library, but I am technically not a volunteer so I imagine I am not granted the same privileges. Dixie can sense my apprehension.

"Dorie, I've told you. No one cares if you eat here with me. Good God. Mrs. Singer keeps a bag of salt and vinegar potato chips in her desk drawer and she's the head librarian."

I walk behind the desk and take out my lunch. Dixie is already in the middle of eating his. He has spread out a large cloth napkin with a red gingham print. On top of the napkin he has a large hunk of bread that is matched in size by a hunk of cheese. There is also a small selection of tiny pickles.

"What are you having?" I ask.

"It's called a ploughman's lunch. I read about it in a biography of Sir Alec Guinness, the famous British actor."

"It looks interesting."

"It is. I'm not sure I like it, but it's important to try new things. If I see something on a menu that I've never had before I always get it. I mean you never know if you are going to like something until you try it, right?" Dixie says, and hands me one of the tiny pickles on his napkin. I take the pickle and pop it in my mouth.

"Mmm. It's good," I say. The only pickles I have ever had were sour and salty. This one tastes sweet and is crunchy.

"So, tell me how is your experiment going?"

"You mean the one for Twenty-Eight Great?" I ask. I'm pretty sure he is asking about Grant and the Holly Trinity, but I don't want to assume anything.

"Dorie, you know I mean your experiment to infiltrate the Holly Trinity. How did studying with Grant go?"

"Well, that's just it. It didn't go."

"He didn't show up?"

"He showed up. He just didn't stay." I explain how Grant came over, scarfed down a few minitacos, and abandoned our project in order to go watch some snowboarding finals at a friend's house down the street.

"Well, that's not good," Dixie says as he tears off a corner of his bread.

"I know. How are we supposed to have completed the research and prototype for the Marconi wireless radio by December if he won't participate?"

"Dorie, that's only half your problem. If you can't get Grant interested in you, then you can't get Grant to dump you."

"And if I can't get Grant to dump me, then I can forget about being a member of the Holly Trinity."

"Exactly."

"But what can I do? I can't get him over to my house and then lock him in closet and force him to ask me out."

"I guess that would be a little too Farrah Fawcett in *Extremities*."

"I assume that's a movie." By now I am getting used to Dixie's constant cinematic references. He nods his head but tells me it is definitely a film I can skip. We sit in silence for a while, both thinking of what the next step should be. After a few minutes, Dixie snaps his fingers.

"I've got it!" he says in a voice loud enough to get us kicked out of the library if we weren't the only two people in it. "WWJGD!" I have no idea what he is talking about.

"Is that a movie?" I ask.

"No, darlin'. You told me that Jane Goodall is your idol, right?"

"Absolutely," I say.

"So, WWJGD stands for 'What Would Jane Goodall Do'?"

"I get it now," I say. Dixie always has so many good ideas. I start thinking about what Jane would do in this situation.

"What would Jane do if she invited one of those monkeys over and he flew the coop?"

"Dixie, they weren't monkeys. They were chimpanzees, and she didn't invite them to London. . . ." As soon as the words start coming out of my mouth, I realize the solution to my problem. I think Dixie does too because he is smiling and nodding. I finish my thought, "She went to Africa to study them."

"Bingo, darlin'!"

"I have to get myself invited over to Grant's to work on the project so I can study him in his own environment."

"More important, if you are at his house, he can't escape."

"Thank you, Dixie. What would I do without your help?"

CHAPTER

18

"What is a weed? A plant whose virtues have
not been discovered." —Ralph Waldo Emerson

I 'm scribbling furiously in my lab notebook, trying
to figure out ways to get invited over to Grant's
house, as Principal Wabash reads through the morning announcements. It's clear Mrs. Wabash did not leave
her up-and-coming career as a radio DJ to become the
principal at Greenview. She tries to be upbeat, but it's
pretty clear she isn't comfortable with this daily chore as
she clears her throat often and constantly mispronounces
things. However, my ears focus in as she finishes up her
speech.

"Now I would like to hand over the microphone to class president Holly McAdams, who has an important message for all of you."

Everyone in homeroom stops what they are working on and gives Holly his or her full attention. When you are the most popular girl in school and the class president, you command that sort of respect.

"Hey, everyone," Holly says. She is as confident as Mrs. Wabash is awkward. Her voice just glides out of the speaker. "The seventh-grade class will be planning the annual Holiday Dance the first week of December. There will be a meeting after school today in the multipurpose room for anyone interested in helping out on any of the committees. Let's make this the best Holiday Dance in Greenview history!"

I applaud at the end of her speech. I was sure everyone else in class would too, but I am the only one. Holly is truly a force of nature. Her enthusiasm for the dance is downright contagious. She could sell snow to Inuits. I can barely wait until the end of school to go to the meeting. I'm sure Alexis and Jenny will be there.

I see Dixie in the hall after homeroom and ask if he is planning to go to the meeting. I make sure none of the boys who usually tease him are around so he won't be self-conscious.

"I don't know," he says. "I'd probably be the only boy there."

"So what? Think how much your style and flair would impress Holly and everyone."

"I don't give a flip about impressing Miss Holly," he says. I feel a little hurt that he is so quick to dismiss my greatest aspiration, but I think he realizes this. "I'm sorry. I mean, you know I totally support your pursuit of popularity."

"I know," I say, and feel a little guilty for feeling even a little hurt. After all, Dixie has bent over backward to help me.

"But maybe you're right," he says, putting his hand on his chin. "I guess the dance committee could use a little of my personal brand of fabulous. I'll meet you there after school."

I wait outside the multipurpose room for Dixie. I'm worried because so far only girls have turned up for the meeting. I've recognized Tara Dowden, Lori Epstein, Moonbeam Williams, Stacey DasGupta, and her twin sister, Leah. As each girl goes in, I wave and smile.

When Dixie arrives, the fact that he is the only boy in the room barely matters. He actually knows a few of the girls from some of his classes and starts talking with them as we wait for the meeting to start.

Holly walks in, followed by Alexis and Jenny, of course. They proceed to the table in the front of the room and Holly begins the meeting after a quick chat with Ms. Garcia, the Spanish teacher who also advises the class council.

"It's great to see so many of you here," Holly says, her smile beaming out into the universe. Indeed there are at least two dozen girls in the room and Dixie, of course. "Putting the dance together is a lot of work, so we will divide responsibility by committee. I will be chairing the entertainment committee. We need about three or four of you to help me select a DJ for the dance and decide what songs will be played. The event will be catered, so we need a few people to help select the caterer and decide what will be served. This is very important. As some of you know, last year there was an incident with some spoiled virgin piña colada mix."

Everyone in the room starts whispering. I guess this was a town scandal last year, but I look over at Dixie and shrug. Since we are both new, this is the first we've heard of it.

"Jenny will be the chair of this committee. Jenny,

please stand." Jenny stands up to identify herself as if there is a single person in the room who does not know who she is.

"Finally, the rest of you will be on the decorations committee. This will be chaired by Alexis. Alexis, please stand." Alexis stands and waves like she is the queen on a parade float. Of the three she is probably the one with the most natural beauty.

Holly goes over the schedule for preparing for the dance and says that the first order of business is to select a theme. "Alexis will write down your ideas on the chalkboard so we can see which idea is the best. Okay, who has an idea?"

I wish I had known she was going to be asking for suggestions. I would have done some research to come up with something. I rack my brain trying to come up with something while a few other girls raise their hands.

"Well, my cousin had a bar mitzvah with a surfing kind of luau theme, and it was really fun 'cause, like, you could wear shorts and flower necklaces and stuff," Lori Epstein says. Holly just looks at her for a second. Alexis goes to write down the suggestion on the chalkboard, but Holly stops her.

"No, don't put that one up." Alexis backs away from the

chalkboard like it is radioactive. "No offense, Lori, but that theme is as old as my grandma. Let's try to come up with something innovative or at least not totally stupid. Oh and by the way, Lori, those flower necklaces are called *leis*."

After Holly's comment most of the girls put their hands down, but I suddenly come up with an idea and put my hand high in the air so Holly will see me.

"Ah, you." Holly says without really pointing at me.

"Me?" I say pointing at myself.

"Ah, yeah. You are the only person with her hand up."

"Oh, okay." I clear my throat and stand up. "My name is Dorie Dilts for those of you who don't know me, and I would like to suggest an ecology theme."

"Did she say biology?" I hear someone whisper.

"What is an ecology theme?" Alexis asks as if I have just suggested the dance's theme be painful dental procedures.

"Ecology is about responding to the diminishing natural resources of the planet like rain forests and wildlife. We could put up posters of endangered animals like the Beluga Whale. We would serve ecofriendly snacks and make sure we all wear ecofriendly green clothing."

"Oh God. I can't wear green!" Alexis says in a panic. "I went to a colorist with my mother, and she said I cannot under any circumstances wear green. It clashes with my skin tone."

"I think she means clothes made of natural fabrics," Jenny says, but this does not calm Alexis down much.

"Yeah, you could wear whatever color you want," I say.

Holly looks at me like I have three heads and gestures to Alexis. "Write it on the board, I guess."

"What?" Lori Epstein yells out. Obviously she thinks her suggestion was on par with mine. Alexis does not immediately approach the chalkboard.

"Look," Holly says, "we have to put something up. Just put both of those up since I also have an idea." Alexis writes down both my idea and Lori's. As soon as she is done, Holly tells everyone her idea.

"Picture this: Winter Wonderland. We cover the entire multipurpose room with big white snow drifts made out of cotton."

"Oh God," Dixie whispers to me.

"Shh," I say.

"Oh, Holly, I think that's perfect," Alexis says, and goes to write the idea on the board.

"I love it," Katherine Fukushima says. "I think we should vote right now."

Alexis and Jenny nod their heads. "Okay. Raise your hand for the luau theme," Holly instructs.

The room is so quiet you could hear a pin drop. Everyone sort of looks over at Lori to see if she will raise her hand, and she doesn't. Alexis goes to the board and puts a big zero next to Lori's idea.

"Next is ecology," Holly says. Alexis starts to write a zero next to my idea without even looking at the group. I rocket my hand from my side and clear my throat so loudly I think they might be able to hear me in the principal's office. Finally I say, "Excuse me." After all, I still think ecology is an excellent theme, if I do say so myself. Why shouldn't I give it my support? Alexis finally turns around, looks at me, rolls her eyes, and says, "One." She writes a one next to "ecology."

"Who votes for Winter Wonderland?" Holly asks the group, and almost everyone's hand shoots up as if there was a prize for being the first hand up. Alexis scans the crowd and then writes "22" on the board.

"Looks like we have a theme. Let's finish by signing up for committees." Everyone races to the sign-up sheets at the front of the room. Dixie goes to sign up for decorations, and I make my way through the crowd of girls to get to the entertainment sign-up sheet. There are already a list of half a dozen names on it by the time Holly gets to me.

"Name?" Holly asks me.

"I'm Dorie."

"Oh, right, the ecology girl." Well, I'm more than just the ecology girl. I hope that doesn't become what I am known for since I am also very interested in physics and chemistry. "Look, this committee is pretty full—you might want to sign up for decorations."

"Oh, but I know a lot about music. In my old school my music teacher gave me the recorder solo when we had our final concert, and a lot of people told me I should keep playing the recorder."

"I don't think we are looking for anyone to play the recorder at the dance."

I should have been clearer. I think she has misunderstood me. "Oh, no. I know that. I was just trying to say that I know a little about music is all. I—"

Holly interrupts me. "There is just no more room on this committee. I think you should try decorations. They need a lot of help."

"Thanks," I say. If the list is full, the list is full. What can I do? I walk over to the decorations sign-up and see that

Dixie is third on the list. At least I will know someone on the committee. As I take the clipboard and begin to print my name, I see Katherine Fukushima come back in. I guess she left to freshen up in the bathroom or something. She goes right over to Holly, and I see Holly put her name on the list she is holding. I want to walk over there and let Katherine know how unfair it is that she is able to be on the committee after I was told it was full. But I don't. I know enough about how things work to know that some people, like Katherine, are beautiful and charming. Being popular for them is just natural. For someone like me popularity is something you have to make happen.

I walk toward the doors of the multipurpose room, but before I walk through them I turn around to observe the whole scene. If Jane Goodall were here she would have a field day observing the social rituals of the seventh grade in Greenview, New Jersey. In fact, I realize I should be having a great time watching the rituals of this social group. However, my observational skills don't satisfy me the way they used to. I don't want to be on the outside looking in anymore. I desperately want to be part of it all.

19

"Facts are stubborn things."

—Alain-René Lesage

My dad drives me to Grant's house before taking Gary to some Saturday practice for some sport. Grant lives on the far edge of town, so there is no possible way I could walk there, and a bus doesn't go within five miles of the place. Grant's house is at the top of Skillman Peak, which is the highest elevation in Greenview. As we drive up the road to the house even Gary is impressed with the incredible view of the valley.

"Hey, Dorkie," he says, "can I come over to your boyfriend's and sled down this hill when it snows?"

"Shut up, Gory. He's NOT my boyfriend."

My dad tries to interrupt the potential fight. "All right, that's enough. Gary, Dorie is going to this boy's house to study. How goes the great Marconi experiment, anyway?"

I explain to my dad how I have pretty much finished all of the preliminary research and that the next steps are going to be more difficult. We need to figure out how we are going to present the material, and then we have to actually build the prototype radio.

"Well, if you need help, let me know. I'm a little better with a microscope than an alkaline battery, but still."

"Thanks, Dad. I think I'll be okay."

"You mean *we*, don't you? Remember, a good scientist knows how to collaborate."

"Of course, Dad," I say, and I look out the window. I don't want to give him a chance to catch my eye and see that I am not exactly telling the truth. I know that scientific collaboration is important, but the truth is, I have done absolutely everything so far. Grant has not lifted a finger. I did ask him to do a little bit of the research, but a week later, when I asked him for the material, he looked at me like I didn't know what I was talking about. That blunder and the fact that he ran out of our first study session has made me reevaluate the collaborative nature of our project. I've simply done all the work myself. While I realize this may be the way to complete the project, it isn't really helping with my larger goal. I basically invited myself over to Grant's using the very minor lie that our dining room is being wallpapered and will be out of commission for the next week or so. It isn't being wallpapered at the moment, but I did hear my mother say she would like to put up new wallpaper in the dining room, so this charade is, in fact, based on something truthful.

Grant's house is so big that my dad is not actually sure where to drop me off. Part of the driveway goes to the back of the house while another section leads to a smaller carriage house. My dad decides to just keep following the one he is on and drops me off at the very front of the house. I get out of the car and approach the huge black double doors and look for the doorbell, but I can't find it. However, each of the doors has a huge brass lion head with a ring in his mouth. I pick up one of the heavy rings and use it to knock on the door. No answer. I look back at my dad, who is still in the car waiting to make sure I am all right, and shrug my shoulders. I'm sure this is the right address and the right time. I'm just about to walk back to the car when the door opens.

"What are you doing at this door?" Grant says with a sneer. I turn around and wave at my father so he can drive off.

"Nice to see you, too, Grant," I say as sarcastically as possible, but I think he thinks I actually mean it. I make a mental note to work on my sarcastic tone more.

I follow Grant past room after empty room. Each one looks like it belongs in a furniture store instead of a house. Everything is perfectly arranged and there is no sign of life anywhere. It's actually a little sad.

"This is where I hang out," Grant says, and opens the door to a room the size of half the first floor of our whole house. It's as much of a mess as the other rooms are spotless. However, it's hard to notice anything except the huge flat-screen TV mounted on the wall.

"I've gone to movie theaters with smaller screens than that," I say, pointing.

"Yeah, it's awesome," Grant says. He is truly proud of the thing whereas I would be a little embarrassed by it. He grabs the remote and starts pressing a few buttons as he explains the millions of features the TV has. "It's almost a year old, so a lot of the features are out of date. I got it last year for my birthday."

"You must have been really good," I say, and Grant laughs.

"It has nothing to do with me being good. My parents skipped my birthday for a cruise of some Greek islands. They felt guilty, so they left me with this."

"Oh," I say, "I'm sorry. That's terrible."

Grant is truly surprised by my reaction. "What are you talking about? It's great. I got my parents out of the house AND I got this awesome television." Grant doesn't even look at me as he talks. He just keeps flipping through the channels. The TV hypnotizes him like a magician in a Bugs Bunny cartoon.

"Are your parents home now?"

"They're out looking at houses with my brother, Daniel, and his fiancée," Grant says, but does not move his eyes from the television.

"Is Daniel the one who is becoming a doctor?" I ask, remembering he mentioned something about this when he was over my house.

"Yeah. Yeah. Yeah," he says, but his voice is no longer dull and monotone. Each word is punctuated with a hint of rage, and he actually turns off the television. Most girls would simply know enough to just change the subject right there, but not me. My scientific curiosity gets the better of me and I ask the question that I know should not be asked.

"Do you not get along with Daniel?"

"Enough already about Daniel. I'm sick of it. Daniel this. Daniel that." He's getting angrier with each word. "Grant," he says in a nasal voice that I assume is suppose to be one of his parents, "you should look up to Daniel. Daniel's getting married. Daniel's buying a house. Daniel's in medical school, and you can barely pass your classes."

Grant's face is bright red. I feel terrible. I should not have asked about his brother, but how was I supposed to know? I have no idea what to do. I just stand there for a second without saying anything. Grant just stares in front of himself. I finally decide to break the silence, "Well, if we work together I'm sure we can get an excellent grade on this science project. That will show your parents."

I have no idea what Grant's reaction will be. I study his face for the slightest change. Suddenly a smile shines across his face. "Hey, that's not a half-bad idea. I knew you were smart in science and everything, but I didn't know you knew about life stuff."

"Thanks," I say.

I show Grant the research I have collected so far and talk him through the basic history of Marconi's invention. He is not exactly fascinated by the topic, but at least he keeps the television off and does not leave the room. This in itself is an incredible improvement.

After an hour or so of studying he says, "I'm starving. Let's get something to eat and take a break."

"But we haven't even covered basic electric impedance," I say, but Grant is already walking out of the room. I guess we have studied enough for one afternoon.

Grant's kitchen looks like it belongs on a Food Network show. There are polished copper pans hanging over the stove, and brand-new appliances shine on top of the dark marble countertops. Grant grabs a tray out of the fridge and pops it in the toaster oven. Then he goes back to the fridge and takes out a small covered bowl. He takes the tray out of the toaster oven, pulls out a fancy plate, and arranges the food and dipping sauce like you would see it in a restaurant. I'm silent during this whole event. I assumed Grant was going to rip open a bag of Cheez Doodles with his teeth. Instead he has prepared these little appetizers and presented them to me. They look a bit familiar. I pick one up and take a bite.

"These are delicious," I say with complete sincerity.

"Thanks," Grant says, replacing his usual cocky tone with a slightly more humble attitude. "I replaced the scallions your mom used with cilantro. I think they came out pretty good."

"Oh, right." I suddenly remember the minitacos my mom served when Grant came over to study. These are almost the same exact snack, but the small change gives the minitacos a more distinct flavor. I might even say these are better than the ones my mom made. But I don't remember my mom giving Grant the recipe. Maybe he found it online. "Where did you get the recipe?"

"I didn't use a recipe," Grant says, his cockiness returning. "The ones your mom made were really good, so I just came home and tried out a few things until I found something that worked."

"These are awesome," I say. He takes a pair of tongs to lift a few more of the tacos from the tray onto my plate and smiles at me.

CHAPTER

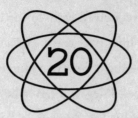

20

"What does not benefit the hive is of no benefit to the bee." —Marcus Aurelius Antonius

Alexis Martinez is truly beautiful. She has long black hair that bounces and shines like she is perpetually auditioning for a shampoo commercial. Her skin is caramel colored, and a pimple wouldn't dare interrupt the smooth surface.

Everything she wears looks like it jumped off the pages of a magazine. Last week I wore the same pair of jeans to school for five straight days. Alexis never seems to wear the same outfit twice. I'm lucky if I get my socks to match each other. Alexis makes sure the color of the pen she uses in class matches her outfit. I can see Alexis through the window in

the door to the classroom where the decorations committee is holding its meeting. She is showing her new shoes to
a few girls who have arrived early to the meeting and they
are oohing and ahhhing over them. For a second I consider
going in and joining the chorus of admirers. However, those
girls are all wannabes. They will never be part of the inner
sanctum of popularity. Yes, I need to have contact with
Alexis, but if I align myself with the mass of girls who want
to be friends with her and the Trinity, I'll simply get lost in
the shuffle. Once I get Grant to dump me, I'll have a guaranteed in and rise above the crowd.

"Hey, darlin'," Dixie says, "why are you staring through
the window?"

"I was just waiting for you to go in. You ready?"

Dixie nods and opens the door. Alexis doesn't even
notice us. We take two seats near the back of the room and
a few more girls come in. I recognize Gwen Thurber from
my Spanish class, and Dixie waves to Tara Dowden from
his algebra class. She sits next to us and Dixie introduces
me. He really is great at meeting people.

"All right, everyone, can I have your attention please?"
Alexis says, patting her hand on the table. Everyone stops
chatting and gives Alexis their attention. I look around the

room and decide that about 60 percent of the people in the room are here to kiss up to Alexis and the other 40 percent are here because they actually want to help with the dance. "The theme for this year's dance is Winter Wonderland. I know it seems like the dance is far off, but really we have only a few weeks." Alexis begins walking around the room like Mrs. Cobrin does during English class. I get a little nervous when she heads to the back of the room near me and Dixie. "Today our job is to come up with ideas for decorations. We'll brainstorm, and I will list suggestions on the board."

Alexis takes the cap off a dry-erase marker and starts taking suggestions. Some kids raise their hands and offer all the usual ideas: snowflakes, snowmen, snow. There is nothing very original and this seems to make Alexis cranky for some reason. "People, look, we need some original ideas here. We want this dance to better than last year's by a mile. We want to basically erase the memory of last year's dance."

Dixie, who has been rather quiet, slowly raises his hand, and Alexis points at him without great expectations. It is incredible how painfully shy Dixie is in groups. "Well," he says quietly, "I think the ideas y'all have come up with are really good, but I think what we are missing is a back story."

"What's that?" Alexis asks with an exasperated sigh.

"Well, it's basically the whole story that the theme is designed around. I've been thinking about Winter Wonderland, and I thought, what if we say that the Snow Queen has placed a spell on the school and transformed the smelly, old multipurpose room into her Winter Wonderland palace? That way instead of just snowmen we could use beads to create icicles and drape some white organza to look like the Snow Queen's royal gown. I have a few sketches."

Dixie takes his notebook out of his bag and opens it to show everyone what he has come up with. The sketches are beautiful, and Alexis is really impressed. Everyone agrees that using the Snow Queen idea as a back story for Winter Wonderland is fantastic. Dixie has really inspired everyone's creativity and the ideas start flying.

Alexis sets a date for the next meeting and says, "I think we have the makings for an awesome dance. This is going to be way better that last year's. Way better. Holly is going to be so psyched."

Everyone starts to leave and I tell Dixie what a great job he did. His friend Tara also tells him she is impressed. "You really saved Alexis's neck," Tara says.

"What do you mean?" I ask as I help Dixie put some of his sketches back in his bag.

"Oh right. The two of you are new. You don't know what happened last year," Tara says.

"What happened?" Dixie asks before I am able to get the question out of my mouth.

"Well," Tara says, and then looks around to make sure no one else is in the room. It feels like she is going to share a very volatile piece of information with us. "Last year Holly was supposed to go to the dance with Grant Bradish. Do you know who he is?"

"Do we ever!" Dixie begins until I give him a gentle kick under the table. Tara seems nice enough, but I don't want to reveal my experiment to her. Dixie gets the hint and says, "I mean, I think I've heard of him."

"Well, Grant dumped Holly the night before the dance. It was the biggest scandal this school has ever seen since they found a lunch lady's hairnet in the lasagna a few years ago."

Dixie and I both stare at Tara with our mouths open.

"My mom is picking me up. I gotta go. Bye," Tara says quickly, and is gone.

I wait until we are entirely alone to speak. "Dixie, do you realize what this means?"

"No more lasagna for lunch?"

"Well that too. But it also means I have to get Grant to

ask me to the dance and then have him dump me before the actual event."

"Exactly."

"But that's only a few weeks away," I say, feeling a small pit develop in my stomach. When I started this experiment I never really considered a hard deadline. Now that I might have one, I feel a little nervous.

"But I thought things were going well," Dixie says.

"They are. I mean, he knows my name and we are even getting some work done for our science project, but getting him to ask me to the dance . . . That seems a bit far off."

Dixie gets up from his chair and waves his arm in the air like is holding a pretend scarf. "Oh *l'amour. L'amour. Toujours l'amour*," he says, and then looks at me expecting a reaction. "You have never seen the movie *The Women*?"

I shake my head.

"Done, I'm officially enrolling you in Silver Screen Romances 101. First session—this weekend. We'll watch *Sleepless in Seattle*, *Ghost*, and *An Affair to Remember*. If those don't give you some ideas about how to get more romantic with Grant, I don't know what will."

"That's a great idea. You bring the DVDs, I'll have my lab notebook, and my mom will make some snacks." I bet

I can learn something from these movies. A good scientist never misses an opportunity to expand her observational skills.

"Dorie, you are probably the only person in the world who would bring a lab notebook to watch movies," Dixie says, and I suddenly feel embarrassed by what I have said until Dixie finishes his statement. "You know, I think it is one of the things I like about you the most."

Dixie comes over to my house and we spend six hours watching movies in the family room. The air has turned crisp and cool, so my dad has a fire burning in the fireplace and my mom has made us some hot mulled apple cider. My parents have both grown to like Dixie and thankfully both of them have realized Dixie is not my boyfriend. I don't know why, but I just could never think of Dixie that way.

Dixie gives a running commentary through each movie. He knows every line and every frame. At the end of each movie he cries and says, "*That* is my favorite movie." After he says that for a third time, I jokingly question his integrity.

"Dixie, you have said that after each movie."

"I know, darlin', but what can I say. After I see each one again it becomes my favorite. Anyway, I'm dying to know what you've learned. I've never looked at any of these movies scientifically before."

I look over my notes to see if there is any earth-shattering conclusion I can share. Unfortunately nothing jumps out at me. "I don't know. A lot of these movies deal with love at first sight and that just seems like a scientific impossibility to me."

"Oh, Dorie, you can't let science limit you. You have to let it open the possibilities. After looking at these movies there must be something you can cook up!"

I stare at my lab notebook. What could I possibly cook up? Then it hits me harder than Rosie O'Donnell hits her punch lines in *Sleepless in Seattle*. "That's it!"

Just then Dixie's mom drives up to the front of our house and toots her horn for Dixie to come out. "What's it?" Dixie asks, desperate to know what I have uncovered before going home.

"It's too long to explain and your Mom's here. I'll tell you about it ipso facto."

"That better mean on the phone when I get home in like seven minutes," Dixie says as he gathers his DVDs and walks to the door.

I wave to Mrs. Finch as she drives Dixie away, and he puts his hand to his ear in the shape of a telephone with one last plea for me to call him. Unfortunately, I've got too much research to do before my study session with Grant tomorrow to do much of anything else but work on the next part of my experiment.

My mom is the perfect person to help me get started. She's reading a book in her bedroom when I burst in with my request. "Mom, I need your best recipe for peanut brittle, fast." I'm so excited by my idea I'm almost out of breath.

"Dorie, what kind of peanut brittle emergency could you be having?" my mom asks peering over her book.

"It's not a peanut brittle emergency. It's a science emergency."

Fifteen minutes later I have my mother's favorite recipe for peanut brittle in my hand and start scribbling in my lab notebook.

Dorie Dilts—November—Lab Report
Objective: To get Grant interested in science.
Materials: Sugar, salt, baking soda, and peanuts.
Methods: Translate the culinary to the scientific.

"Language is only the instrument of science,
and words are but the signs of ideas."
—Samuel Johnson

Before getting to Grant's house to work on our project, I ask my Mom to stop at the grocery store so I can pick up some of the things we will need. Most of the materials are pretty common, but I don't want to show up at Grant's and find out he doesn't have something we need.

Grant opens the door and pushes some of his blond hair away from his eyes. "What is all this? I thought you said we absolutely had to start working on the lab report no matter how boring it is."

I walk past Grant confidently. I just know this is going to get him interested in science, and once I do that I can get him to ask me to the dance. The one thing all of those movies had in common was that each of the couples shared a passion for something. "The kitchen is that way, right?" I ask.

"Yeah," Grant says confused, "but the computer and books and stuff are in the library. Have I been that bad an influence on you? You giving up on the whole experiment?"

"Not at all." I don't even look back as I head down the hall to the kitchen. For some reason, I know Grant will follow me.

I put the bags of groceries on the counter and start taking out the materials. Grant starts looking over what I have purchased. "Hey, if you want to cook instead of writing up a lab report procedures, that's cool with me."

"Actually, we are going to do both."

"Huh?"

"Grant, you like to cook, right?"

Grant shrugs his shoulders as if he could care less about cooking. I just look at him for a moment and realize how exhausting it must be to keep up the cool image all day, every day.

"I'm not gonna tell anybody," I say, and Grant finally surrenders.

"Yeah, I like to cook. So what?"

"So, cooking is really just science using food ingredients instead of lab samples and frying pans instead of test tubes. When you think about it, what is a stove really but a modified Bunsen burner."

"Great," he says in a voice layered with sarcasm, "you've found a way to make cooking boring."

"No," I say, "I've found a way to make science edible." I take out my lab notebook and show him the translated recipe. "We are going to make a partial thermal degradation of carbon dioxide foamed saccharides with protein inclusions," I say letting the complex words roll off my tongue very matter-of-factly.

"WHAT?" Grant says like I have been speaking in a Martian tongue.

"Oh, no," I say with mock concern, "I hope you aren't allergic to protein inclusions, because we can leave those out if you are."

"What the hell are protein inclusions?" Grant asks. I grab the bag of peanuts off the counter and throw them at him. He catches them easily, as one would expect the star of the

Greenview basketball team to do. "These are peanuts," he says, confused.

"I know but when you describe them on a lab report you would call them by a more scientific name, like protein inclusions. See, I've turned my mother's recipe for peanut brittle into a lab report."

He looks carefully at the page of my notebook. He struggles trying to figure it all out for a few seconds, and then he says, "Oh, so where you should have a list of ingredients you have a list of materials."

"Exactly," I say. I wonder if this is what teachers feel like when they really get through to some kid.

"But what are all these things?"

I take out a Post-it pad from my backpack and start labeling all of the ingredients so that Grant can see the scientific names of each item. I put SUCROSE on the bag of sugar, SOLIDIFIED ESTERS on the butter, and SODIUM CHLORIDE on the salt. Grant examines each label. I show him how a recipe is really just a lab report with a list of materials and procedures. Whereas a recipe might say "measure out a cup of sugar," a list of procedures in a lab report would say "mass out 75g of sucrose," but the result would be the same.

Grant is actually interested in the recipe/lab report. He

looks it over carefully and before we begin he says, "You know we could substitute a different variety of protein inclusions."

"Variation is the basis for scientific exploration. What have you got?"

Grant opens one of the cabinets next to the sink and pulls out a jar of cashews. "What do you think of these protein inclusions? I believe they have been prepared without sodium chloride, which is what the recipe," he catches himself before continuing, "which is what the *lab report* specifies."

Grant laughs, and I laugh with him. For the first time since we have met he seems so relaxed and easygoing. He isn't the cocky, bored kid in the back of the classroom cracking jokes. He's nice and he's able to laugh at himself. I like this side of Grant so much better than the jerk I see at school.

We work through the procedures together. He stirs the sticky concoction carefully as we both stare at the candy thermometer waiting for the mixture to reach the proper temperature. I explain that adding the baking soda, aka sodium bicarbonate, will create a chemical reaction.

I stir and he carefully measures out the remaining ingredients. We take the pot off of the stove as per the lab procedures, and Grant adds the white powder. Suddenly the whole mixture foams due to the chemical reaction.

"Cool," Grant says, and he holds the tray we greased with solidified esters as I pour the candy onto it.

As we wait for the candy to cool I consider suggesting we start working on more of our actual homework, but I don't want to interrupt the mood we have going. Grant, who usually maintains a conversation with a series of grunts and head nods, is actually talking in full sentences. He tells me how he started cooking for himself since his parents weren't often home for dinner. He tells me about some of his favorite things to cook (chocolate chip cookies, chicken fingers, and chili), and I tell him about my idol, Jane Goodall.

Before we know it, the brittle is cool enough to eat. He breaks off a piece and offers it to me. At first I just reach for it without thinking, but as soon as my eyes meet his everything stops. Grant is certainly very cute and for a second I really see him. I see this nice guy looking at me, and really seeing me, and offering me a piece of candy that we just made together. Something has changed from the friendly banter of just a few minutes ago. I wish I could take a picture of the moment and put that image under a microscope to examine the ether. My hand comes up from my side and I watch my arm move toward Grant in almost slow motion when—

"Grant! Grant!" I hear someone scream from another room. Grant is actually startled enough to drop the piece of candy on the floor. Could he have been caught in the same moment I was? "Grant! Grant!" The voice is closer and angrier now.

"I'm in the kitchen!" Grant hollers back while quickly grabbing a paper towel to clean up the spilled candy. I hear heels clicking along the polished wood floor in the hall outside the kitchen, then a beautiful woman about my mom's age and dressed in a tweed suit with brown velvet trim appears. I assume this is Grant's mother.

"Grant," the woman says exasperated, "I've been calling and calling your name. I wanted to let you know that I'm home, but I am going to meet a business associate of your father's for dinner." At first Mrs. Bradish doesn't even see me, though I am only a few feet away from her. "Oh, who is this girl?" she asks as if I am not in the room.

"This is Dorie," Grant says.

"Hello," I say, and hold up the tray of candy. "Would you like some partial thermal degradation of carbon dioxide foamed saccharides with protein inclusions?"

"Excuse me?" she says, holding her hand to her chest.

"It's just a scientific name for peanut brittle. It's my mother's recipe, but I translated it. I think it turned out pretty good."

"Scientific name? Very impressive," Mrs. Bradish purrs, and gives me a once-over. I have passed whatever secret test parents give kids to make sure they are all right.

"Yeah. I substituted cashew for the stated protein inclusion," Grant adds, but his mother barely hears him. She is too busy examining me silently. I feel funny with her looking at me.

"To think, I assumed you were Grant's girlfriend, but I can't imagine he understood any of what you said. Grant's grades are not exactly honor-roll material," she says, staring at Grant. Her eyes throw each word at him like a tiny dagger. I can't believe a mother would say something like this about her son in front of someone she has just met. I wonder if she has been drinking, and then I smell the alcohol on her breath. I look over at Grant. He is furious, hurt, and embarrassed. He looks at his mother with contempt. I wish I were not here. I wish I had worked harder on my invisibility machine when I was nine.

Grant's eyes narrow and he walks closer to me and his mother. I think he is about to yell at her or scream or something. Instead he puts his arm around me and tells his mother, "As a matter of fact, she IS my girlfriend. How do you like that? She doesn't think I'm stupid."

I freeze. I'm actually frozen in space. I think if someone were to pull at my leg it would just snap off.

"Oh, Grant," Mrs. Bradish says, waving her hand across her face. This makes the smell of the alcohol on her breath more noticeable. "No one said you were stupid. I just don't see how you are going to get into meadichol skwool if you . . ." Her last few words are slurred and she trails off before finishing. She starts walking away from the kitchen, but before she leaves she stops suddenly and turns around.

"Well," she says, staring at Grant again, her voice full of contempt, "if this *is* your girlfriend, I guess we can expect to see her at your brother's wedding next month. Good. I wanted there to be someone there your age so at least there would be someone for you to talk to. I don't want you hanging around your brother, ruining his day." She turns back around, stumbles a bit, and then walks out of the kitchen.

I don't say anything. I stare at the floor, but out of the corner of my eye I can see Grant's face is bright red. I am not sure if he is flushing due to embarrassment or anger, or both. There is a long awkward silence then Grant suddenly speaks.

"I'm going to play Xbox," he says as if nothing has happened. He walks right past me, leaves the kitchen, and heads down the hall. There are still dirty bowls and pans to be cleaned, and he hasn't even tasted the candy. I grab my notebook and head down the hall after him. By the time I get to the doorway he has already turned on the television and is staring at it, holding the game controller waiting for the game to load. I wait for a second, assuming he will say something about what just happened, but he doesn't. He just stares at the huge television, pressing the buttons on his game controller with such intensity that I think it might break.

"Grant," I finally say, hoping to get his attention, but he ignores me. I try again louder. "Grant!"

This time I have gotten his attention. He roars back at me, "WHAT DO YOU WANT?"

I know he is upset, but I haven't done anything wrong. "Don't yell at me. I haven't done anything wrong. You are the one who just told your mother I'm your . . ." I can't actually say it out loud. I stop short, but I'm sure he gets what I am trying to say.

"Look, my brother's wedding is, like, the first week in December, and now you, like, *have to* go with me to keep my mom off my back."

"Excuse me?" I say. Now I am the one getting angry. I move between Grant and the television to block his view.

"I can't see the TV," he whines.

"*Have to go with you to the wedding?* I don't *have to* do anything. I don't take orders very well. I am an independent young woman."

"Look, I told my mom you are coming, so you gotta go so she will think you are my girlfriend or something. It's the first week of December."

It's like he hasn't heard a word I said. When he says "first week of December" a second time that date suddenly clicks in my head as a very important one, and I remember why. "That's the weekend of the school dance," I say.

"Oh, great," he says sarcastically. "I guess that means I'll have to take you to the dance also so my mom isn't suspicious. Me and my big mouth."

"Listen, Grant, if you think you can tell me what to do you can think again." This time I am the one almost shouting. "I am not going to—" Then like a car braking as a deer appears in the headlights, I stop. What am I doing? Grant just said he was going to take me to the dance. He said he was going to take me to the dance so that he can pretend to be my boyfriend. I did it. I can't believe it. I'm as good as popular.

CHAPTER

22

"If you cannot, in the long run, tell everyone what you have been doing, your doing has been worthless."
—Theodor Ambrose Hubert Schwann

I eat so many of my lunches in the library with Dixie that I feel like I work there too. I was planning on actually eating in the cafeteria today, but Dixie insisted I join him since we don't have any classes together and he claims he will literally explode if he does not find out what happened with Grant. I tried to explain to him before homeroom that it would be scientifically impossible for him to physically explode without the assistance of some type of chemical reaction, but he was uninterested in my theory.

Dixie is waiting behind the desk for me like I am a book that is way overdue. "Hey, Dixie, how is school going today?"

"No, no, no, no, no. Don't even try to change the subject or waste time finding out how Seth Perkins threw a spitball at me during gym that stuck to the back of my head."

"He what? You should tell Coach Hughes. I'm sure—"

"Shush. I don't want to talk about me. I want to talk about you. It will take my mind off the great spitball wizard."

I know Dixie gets teased at lot during class. I haven't actually seen it happen, but everyone knows about it. Seth Perkins is your typical bully. If I ever got the chance, I would punch him right in the face if I saw him hurting Dixie in any way. However, I know it only makes Dixie more upset to talk about it, so instead I do as he asks and give him every single detail of my last meeting with Grant. He laughs in all the right places and asks a million questions to get more details. When I get to the denouement of the story, Dixie actually chokes on his watercress and salmon cracker.

"He actually told his mother you are his girlfriend?" he manages to ask between coughs.

"Dixie, drink something or you'll choke."

He grabs his Orangina bottle and pours some into his glass. "Choke? Please. I'm about to have a heart attack. Can a thirteen-year-old have a heart attack? He actually called you his girlfriend?"

"Wait. It gets better. I'm going with him to his brother's wedding, and he's taking me to the Winter Wonderland dance."

"WHAT? Dorie, you accomplished more on a Saturday afternoon than I did all week. I barely managed to deep condition my hair. Do you think Grant might, you know?"

I have no clue what Dixie is hinting at. "You know, what?"

"Dorie, do I have to spell it out for you? Do you think Grant might, you know, like you, like you."

I can't believe Dixie would even ask me such a thing. "Are you kidding? There is no possible way he could or would. I mean, we were actually having a good time making the candy, but as soon as his mom left he turned right back into the arrogant, self-involved object of my experimentation."

"Well, I'm just saying you should—"

"Dixie, I have to focus on the next step of the experiment."

"What's that?"

"Osmosis," I say, knowing Dixie may not know exactly what I mean.

"I'll repeat the question: What's that?"

I explain to Dixie how osmosis is the scientific principle of how water moves from a high concentration to a lower concentration by spreading out, around, and across an environment.

"I get it," he says. "We need to get the word out that you and Grant are an item."

"Exactly," I say. "Are you planning on going to the big dance committee meeting after school on Thursday?"

"I am now," Dixie says, and we begin planning Operation Osmosis.

Dorie Dilts—November—Lab Report
Objective: To spread the word about Dorie and Grant.
Materials: Tara Dowden, dance committee members.
Methods: Osmosis.

On Thursday we meet outside the multipurpose room before going into the meeting. Dixie and I have decided to use this as an opportunity to get the word out. When Dixie arrives, he confirms that our plan is in place.

"I saw Tara Dowden before American history this afternoon, and she said she was going to be here and that Jenny told her the meeting was mandatory for everyone, even kids on the refreshments committee."

"Perfect. Everyone knows Tara Dowden is the thinnest possible membrane to penetrate."

Dixie just looks at me. "Dorie, darlin', English please."

"I'm just saying that Tara is the biggest gossip at Greenview."

"None bigger," Dixie says, and we open the doors to the multipurpose room. As expected Tara is already busily working on making some beaded icicles with Jenny. She is talking a mile a minute while Jenny strings beads and nods. I scan the room to see what Holly is doing. I can't find her.

"Do you see Holly?" I ask Dixie. He shakes his head.

"You are both late," Alexis says.

"Hello to you too," Dixie says.

Alexis ignores his snide comment and gets right to work. "We need the two of you to work on snowflakes. I'll demonstrate the technique and the look we are going for." Alexis walks us over to a large table where some other kids are already hard at work. There is a stack of bright white paper, probably snatched from the copy machine, and a recycled coffee can full of those little scissors you used to get in grade school. Alexis grabs a few pieces of paper and a pair of scissors. She starts folding the paper together and says, "We want these to be very delicate. Think lots of small intricate cuts like this." She uses the scissors to cut through the sheets, and as soon as I see her doing this I interrupt.

"Wait!" I say.

"What's wrong?" Alexis asks. She clearly does not like to be interrupted.

"Well, if you do it that way you'll be cutting through all of the sheets of paper."

"Yeah, I know, duh," she says, continuing to cut.

"Wait!"

"WHAT?" Alexis is truly getting annoyed, but I am sure once I point out the problem she will be grateful for my assistance.

"If you do it that way it means you'll have three snowflakes exactly alike."

"So?" Alexis says. I was hoping pointing out that small detail would be enough for her to see the error of her ways.

"Well that would be scientifically inaccurate. Snowflakes are formed through a complex crystallization process that happens when water vaporizes. It would be virtually impossible for two snowflakes to be exactly alike."

Everyone who is in earshot who had been furiously working on cutting out snowflakes stops and looks at me. Alexis literally has her mouth open. Dixie just smiles at everyone.

"This is not," Alexis begins slowly and deliberately, "a PBS documentary. This is a school dance. We need to make more than five hundred snowflakes before the after-school bus takes off at four thirty." Alexis hands me her scissors and a stack of white paper. She turns on her heel and does not look back. I shrug and start working on cutting out a few flakes. Alexis is the head of the committee, and if she doesn't mind the meteorological inaccuracies, who am I to complain?

After about a half hour of cutting, my hands are sore. After we are done with each snowflake, or rather cluster of scientifically impossible snowflake *clones*, we are supposed to put them in a big box at the end of the table. My contribution stands out conspicuously. Whereas most of the snowflakes look lacey, mine look lumpy. Dixie's are absolutely stunning. Each one is a masterpiece.

I see Alexis coming over, and I take a few of my snowflakes from the top of the pile and shove them to the bottom. She inspects our work briefly and then Dixie turns to her.

"Alexis, I noticed the icicle group is making each piece too long. We don't want them to hit people in the head as they come in," Dixie says. I look over at him slyly, knowing he is implementing Operation Osmosis.

"Oh, no. Dixie, go over and show them how long they should be."

Dixie gets up from the snowflake table and winks at me before heading over to the icicles and Tara Dowden. I continue to cut out snowflakes, but the whole time I have my eyes glued to the icicle group. I see Dixie talking with Tara and then he gets closer to her, like he is almost whispering something in her ear. Then I see him point over at me. I try to pretend like I am really concentrating on my cuts so as not to give him away. Then Tara shakes her head and points at me also. Dixie gets up and walks back over to the snowflakes. As he passes me he doesn't make eye contact but says under his breath, "Operation Osmosis has begun."

We both pretend to work on our snowflakes as we watch everything unfold. Tara gets up and walks over to Alexis, who is inspecting another group. There is a bit of whispering and a bit of pointing in my general direction but nothing too obvious. While Tara makes her way to the other groups, Alexis goes directly to Jenny. Alexis whispers to Jenny, and Jenny gasps. The two of them chat for a second longer, and then Alexis pulls out her cell phone and makes what looks like a very urgent call. I'm sure they will tell Holly, but if only she were here I could make sure. Tara floats from group to group slowly making her way back to the icicles.

"Looks like everything is going according to plan," Dixie whispers to me.

Then the multipurpose room doors fly open. Holly appears, cell phone in hand. She eyes Alexis, who is also on her phone. After a second I realize they are talking to each other. They each snap their cell phones closed at the same time. The Holly Trinity is united. Holly gets a quick briefing from Alexis and Jenny. I can't hear anything they are saying, but I can see the conversation and at one point I can see Holly mouth "WHO?" with a look of confusion and perhaps a hint of anger. Then Jenny and Alexis point over at me. My heart is racing so fast I can barely contain it.

Dixie, who is watching the whole exchange as carefully

as I am, whispers to me, "Do NOT look at them. Do NOT look up." I stay as focused on my snowflake as I possibly can. I strain my eyeball to move all the way to the side of my eye so I can continue to catch a glimpse, then it happens. I see Jenny and Alexis both point at me for Holly to see. The entire Holly Trinity is looking at me. They are actually looking right at me, Dorie Dilts.

CHAPTER

"In completing one discovery we never fail to
get an imperfect knowledge of others."
—Joseph Priestley

The fact that Grant has completely avoided and
ignored me since proclaiming me his girlfriend to
his mother, inviting me to his brother's wedding,
and agreeing to go with me to the dance is not unexpected.
Sure, I was able to briefly see a side of Grant that wasn't a
complete jerk, but as any student of geometry will tell you,
one side of a defined shape does not a polygon make.

I put my books in my locker before homeroom and put
up the small mirror I brought from home. I've always seen
girls with locker mirrors before and thought they were so

stupid. I mean, there are mirrors in the girls' room if you are desperate to see an image of yourself. However, since the whole Grant thing, I've decided I need to keep up a bit of an appearance in order to maintain a level of believability.

"Hey," someone says, and taps me on the shoulder. I turn around and it's Grant. While his personality leaves something to be desired, his physical presence does not. He is definitely one of the cutest, if not the cutest, boys at Greenview. For a split second—not even a split second, a millisecond—I imagine what it would be like if Grant really was my boyfriend and we were really going to the dance together.

"Yo, are you here or out in space or something?" Grant asks, and waves his hand in front of me.

"Space travel is incredibly difficult, Grant."

"It's just something people say. I just wanted to know if we were gonna work on the stupid science project this weekend."

This is quite a change—Grant asking me if we are going to study. In the past I have had to launch an all-out campaign just to get him to return an e-mail about studying. It seems like my little Cooking with Science episode has bitten somebody with the science bug.

"I guess so," I say coyly. I guess I learned something from all of those romantic comedies Dixie made me watch. I finish putting my books in my locker, close the door, and lean against it. The first bell for school rings, which means I have only six minutes until I need to be in homeroom. Some kids head off, and as the crowd thins I spot the Holly Trinity down the hall. Holly walks in the middle, her blond hair flowing, her confidence palpable.

I decide to use this exact moment to turn up the heat a little by deploying my most recent brainstorm. If there's one thing that Sandra Bullock movies from the nineties have in common with the most recent astronomical discussions, it's that sometimes you think you are looking at a star but really all you have in front you is a bunch of combustible gas. If I can execute my experiment with absolute precision, I might make Holly think she's seeing something that's just not there.

Instead of outright saying to Grant, "See you this weekend," I stare down at the ground and mumble some inaudible phrase that I know he will not be able to understand.

"Hummy bum weeky dum," I say through loose lips.

"Huh?"

The Holly Trinity approaches. They are in visual range. I repeat my gibberish.

"Hummy bum weeky dum," I say through loose lips, but this time I take the volume down 50 percent so I know Grant can't hear me. The Trinity is only a few yards away but behind Grant so he cannot see them. Since Grant can't hear me he leans in closer to me and puts his hand over my head on the door of my locker. The Trinity is within earshot. I maneuver quickly from underneath Grant's arm and speak loudly and clearly so that each of them can hear me. "Grant," I say doing my best Drew Barrymore impression, "not here at school. Later." I add a playful Julia Roberts giggle. Dixie will be so proud.

Grant, however, is totally confused. He just says, "See you later, Dorie," and walks away, unaware of the audience that has been carefully following the last few minutes of our exchange. I pretend not to notice their presence as well. I pretend I am adjusting some uncooperative part of my backpack. I pretend I didn't make it look like Grant was about to kiss me.

Holly stands right in front of me. I remind myself to play it cool. People don't like desperation. I don't need to do anything to make Holly like me. I have science on my side. I just need to let the experiment play itself out. But it's hard to remain calm when the most popular girl at school is standing right in front of you with her two best friends and you are on the brink of becoming the third.

Holly says, "You're Doris." It's not a question. It's a statement. I don't correct her; I just nod. Alexis then whispers in her ear. Then Holly says, "You're Dorie." This time I smile and nod.

"Listen, Dorie, I know we don't know each other, but I'm Holly and this is Jenny and Alexis." Is she kidding? In what dimension would Holly need to introduce herself to anyone at Greenview. It's like George Washington saying, "Hi, I'm George. You may not recognize me, though I'm on all the money in your wallet."

"I'm Dorie," I say.

"Yeah," she says like I've said something incredibly stupid, and as soon as the words are out of my mouth, I realize I have. "I just called you Dorie." Part of me wants to say, "Actually you called me Doris," but I remain quiet.

"We saw Grant Bradish trying to kiss you just now." Inside I am going YES YES YES. It worked. It worked. It looked like he was moving closer to kiss me.

"And," Alexis adds, "there is a rumor that he has asked you to the dance."

"It's more than a rumor," Jenny says. "The entire track team knows about it."

Bless you, Tara Dowden, bless you.

I try to play dumb. "Oh, really?" I say all wide-eyed and innocent.

"You're new here so you don't know the lay of the land. I think it's my duty to let you know that Grant has a bit of a reputation," Holly says.

"He does?" I say. Again same wide-eyed innocence. Little do they know I have a lab notebook full of information on his reputation not to mention each of them.

"Grant is a complete jerk. He's such a . . ." Jenny starts going off on Grant. You can tell she is about to explode, but Holly puts up her hand and Jenny gets the message. She grinds her rant to a halt.

"I'm not going to bad-mouth anyone," Holly says. I knew she was a nice person. I can't wait until we are friends. "Not even someone who is as much of a jerk as that idiot Grant. I just won't do it."

"That's very nice of you," I say.

"I know," she says, smiling brightly, almost pleased with her own kindness. "Grant seems really cool, and I'll admit he is hot, but he just uses girls, Dorie."

"He does?" This one is harder to make believable since anyone who has spent more than eight seconds with Grant can see this potential.

Holly opens her purse and pulls out a small piece of paper. "I'm just saying when he breaks your heart, give me a call. I've been there. We've all been there." She hands me the piece of paper and walks away with a quick wave.

I look down in my hand and see the small piece of folded lavender notepaper. I open it up and there in sky blue glitter-gel ink is Holly's name and phone number. I look at the first three numbers and I realize it's not just the number to her parents' landline. It's her actual cell phone number. Oh my God. I have Holly McAdams's cell phone number in my hand. I just stare down at it. I can't believe it. I could probably sell it on eBay and finance my entire college education. But you can't but a price on something like this. Now all I need is a reason to use it.

CHAPTER

"If you thought that science was certain—
well, that is just an error on your part."
—Richard P. Feynman

B ut Dorie, the problem is, you don't have a reason to
use it," Dixie says over the phone. I can hear his
favorite soap opera, *The Bold and the Beautiful*, playing in the background.

"Not yet," I tell him, adjusting the cushions on the
couch in such a way as to allow my head to hang over
the edge without falling over. I can feel the warmth from
the fireplace, and the orange flames make the family room
glow with a cozy warmth.

I never realized how addictive talking on the phone can

be. Dixie and I see each other at school, but still we pretty much talk on the phone every day. Mostly we talk about the experiment, but we also talk about things like what we want to do in the future. We both absolutely love the musical *Wicked*, and we wind up talking about that a lot. "Dixie, there is absolutely no way Grant is going to make good on his promise to take me to the dance. It's only a matter of days until he dumps me."

"Maybe he—," Dixie begins, but I don't let him finish.

"Dixie, I know what you are going to say, and it is just not possible. Grant does not like me." As the words come out of my mouth I review the last few interactions with Grant. The edge of indifference may have worn away a bit, but he still does not treat me with any type of interest. The fact that he regards me without contempt only indicates that he knows how to act civilly toward a girl, nothing else.

"Still, isn't the scientific motto 'Be prepared'?"

"Dixie, that's the Boy Scouts."

"I'm just saying you had better think about how you can get dumped because if you are the only one to make it to a major social event with Grant, you won't be welcomed by the Holly Trinity. You'll be attacked."

Dixie does have a point. After all, I've accomplished the

most important part. Everyone now knows that Grant is supposed to take me to the dance. There is really no point in prolonging this. The sooner I get dumped, the sooner I'm in.

"Maybe you're right, Dixie. But I can't just go up to him and say 'I don't want you to take me to the dance.'"

Dixie gasps deeply before speaking. "Oh my God. No. If you do that, it means you will have dumped him."

"Exactly, and if Holly finds out I did what she couldn't, I'll be ostracized forever."

"Well, at least until eleventh grade."

"What could I do that would really make Grant want to break up with me?"

Dixie and I spend the better part of an hour trying to come up with ideas. Some ideas are just too expensive, like hiring someone to skywrite "Dorie plus Grant" over Greenview.

My parents knock on the wall of the family room before coming in since there is no actual door. "Dorie, sorry to bother you," my mom says.

"Yeah?" I say, and cover the mouthpiece of the phone.

"Are you going to be on the phone much longer?" my dad asks. "Your mom and I are going up to bed."

"But it's only like nine o'clock," I say. My dad puts his

arm around my mom, and they both giggle. Oh, God. I just know I am going to find a trail of romantic Post-it notes in the kitchen tomorrow.

"Tell you what. I'll come down later and smother the fire before everyone goes to sleep," my dad says.

"You'll what?" I shout, and leap up from the couch.

"Smother the fire, Dorie, so the flame doesn't burn all night," my dad says very slowly, not knowing why I have had such a strong reaction. He doesn't realize that he has just given me the perfect scientific solution to my problem. I get up from the couch and hug them good night. Once they are out of the room I pick up the phone, hoping Dixie has not hung up.

"Dixie, are you there?"

"Yep."

Then I introduce my idea to Dixie, "Guys don't like to be smothered, right?"

"You mean in their sleep with a pillow? As a general rule I think they don't like that, but I don't think it's gender specific."

"No, silly. I mean smothered in not giving them their personal space. Scientifically the best way to extinguish a flame is to smother it."

"Oh, I get it. Yeah, guys hate that."

I grab my backpack and pull out the weekly school bulletin and check the athletics schedule. The Greenview basketball team has a home game Thursday night. "How many basketball cheers do you think I could learn by Thursday night?" I tell Dixie my plan, and start writing in my notebook.

Dorie Dilts—November—Lab Report
Objective: To smother Grant (emotionally).
Materials: Greenview spirit paraphernalia, including but not limited to pom-poms, posters, confetti, megaphone.
Methods: Show excessive amount of school spirit and enthusiasm.

The Greenview gym looks like every other school gym in the country. There are polished wood floors, sports banners hanging from the ceiling, and bleachers. By the time I arrive the game has already begun. I wanted to get to the game earlier, but my huge bag of props was harder to carry to school than I thought. I'm not sure if there is a certain side I should sit on since I know next to nothing about basketball. I decide to grab a seat in the middle of the bleachers. Since it isn't so crowded I can move at any point. I lug my bag of props and plop myself down. Grant is already playing in the game. He runs up and down the court, and the whole time his eyes are focused directly on the ball. I imagine if he spent even a fraction of this energy on his schoolwork, he would be one of the smartest kids at school.

I look through my bag and make sure I have everything. I'm going to cheer Grant on with so much enthusiasm that by the end of the game I expect he will not only dump me, but also run away from me. The added bonus is that this all goes down in a very public place. Granted none of the Holly Trinity is here, but Tara Dowden is so it will definitely get back to them.

I take out the "Go, Grant, Go!" poster I made last night and stick the green foam number one finger I bought at the dollar store on my hand. I leave the green and white pom-poms and other props for later. I also have a handful of confetti at the ready if Grant makes a basket. I listen closely to the announcer as he explains the game for the Greenview Internet radio audience. "Greenview steals the ball, Davey Haskell, number thirty-two, passes it to Grant Bradish, number sixteen." As soon as I hear Grant's name, I leap up from seat and start cheering and waving my sign. Grant is so focused on the game that he doesn't even see me until the buzzer sounds announcing that something is out of bounds. The action on the court stops for a moment, and Grant sees me out of the corner of his eye. Even though he doesn't acknowledge me, I know he sees me.

I spend the rest of the game hollering Grant's name and cheering on the team. I wave my big number one finger in the air and hold up different posters as encouragement, and every time Grant makes a basket I throw a wad of confetti in the air. In the beginning I had to fake my enthusiasm, but by the end of the game I am actually really into it. I don't need to fake anything. The last few minutes of the game are entirely gripping. Greenview is down by one point and in the last thirty seconds of the game Rodger Alden makes a basket from outside the three-point line and wins the game. Everyone in the bleachers leaps to their feet cheering. It's very exciting, but I try to regain my composure as I make my way down the bleachers to Grant. I'm sure he saw my overly enthusiastic display of adoration and that this has caused him to go running for the hills. As I make my way to him I wonder if I should cry when he dumps me. That would make the whole thing look very authentic, but I am not sure I have the theatrical ability to cry on cue.

Before I even reach the bottom of the bleachers Grant spots me and walks over to where I am. I can't tell if he's angry or upset from the look on his face. He mostly looks sweaty. At any rate, let the dumping begin.

"Hi, Grant. It sure was fun watching the game. Did you see me in the stands? I had the 'Go, Grant, Go' poster."

"Yeah, I saw you," he says in a low voice. "I want to talk to you about that."

Here it comes. Grant is going to dump me. I just look at him innocently like I have no idea what he is going to say, like I don't know he is going to tell me to back off and leave him alone. I slowly close my eyes in preparation like making a wish when you blow out the candles on a birthday cake.

"Thanks," Grant says.

WHAT? Thanks? I must have heard him wrong. I open my eyes. I shake my head in disbelief. "What did you say?" I ask.

"I wanted to thank you for showing up to the game and cheering me on. No one has ever done that before," he says with a hint of shyness. I am speechless. I don't know what to say.

Coach Snyder barks from basketball court, "Bradish, post game powwow in the locker room. Now." He adds with a slightly mocking tone, "You can talk to your girl-friend later."

Grant snaps to attention and heads back to the locker room but shouts back to me, "See you this weekend so we can work on the science thing."

"Great!" I say in a knee-jerk reaction, but this is anything but great. I gather my posters and props, and brush some of the confetti off my hair before heading back home.

I spend the rest of the night putting together what I think will be the dirty bomb of young relationships. I pick each element carefully and even package the whole thing in such a way as to guarantee full effect. When I get to school the next morning I make sure I get a chance to see Grant before homeroom.

"Hey, Grant," I say, "I have something for you." I pull out the small package wrapped in purple Mylar and covered with lavender bows and pink heart stickers. I wave it around a bit before handing it to him, hoping others will notice the ostentatious display of affection.

"What is it?" Grant asks, looking at the dangling ribbon atop the shiny package.

"It's a mix CD. I put on a bunch of songs that I just know you will love. Open it," I say. I have made sure that each song I have selected would send a diabetic into shock. There is a healthy serving of Céline Dion, with a side order of Hilary Duff, and a liberal sprinkling of ballads from my CD "Broadway Love Songs." If that isn't enough to make him run away, I'm not sure what I'll do next.

Grant waits until more people have cleared the hall before opening the package. I wait patiently knowing he will be disgusted. He rips open the CD and turns it over to look at the list of songs.

"What?" he says looking furtively down the hall. "That big mouth Doug." Now I am the one confused. What does his idiot best friend Doug have to do with this? "Did he tell you? Who else did he tell?" Grant actually looks a bit angry. This is not the reaction I was expecting.

"I don't know what you are talking about. Doug didn't tell me anything."

Grant exhales and looks relieved. "Really?" he says, his mood much lighter. "How did you know my favorite movie is *Titanic*?"

"What?" Are you kidding me? His favorite movie is a period romance? How is it possible that this cocky slacker has more of a soft side than I had possibly accounted for?

"Yeah, and I don't even have this version of 'My Heart Will Go On.' We can play it this weekend when we study. See ya," he says as he stuffs the CD into his backpack and walks away toward his homeroom.

During lunch Dixie and I try to come up with a new plan.

"I still think you need to try smothering him," Dixie says.

"But the basketball game smothering plan was a total failure," I say, digging my plastic spoon deeper into my near-empty cup of blueberry yogurt.

"What do these three people have in common: Katharine Hepburn, Spencer Tracy, and Sidney Poitier?" Dixie asks.

"They are all actors in movies I have never heard of."

"True. But not the answer I'm looking for. They each star in *Guess Who's Coming to Dinner*, or in your case, Guess Who's NOT Coming to Dinner?"

"You think I should invite him to dinner? How is that going to make him dump me?"

"Dorie, not just any dinner. Thanksgiving is next week. You tell Grant how much you want him to come have dinner with your parents and how he absolutely, positively must come to Thanksgiving at your house. I tell you, the very idea of having a formal Thanksgiving dinner with a girl's parents will make him dump you faster than MGM dumped Joan Crawford right before *Mildred Pierce*."

"Dixie, you are brilliant. You're remote control is permanently stuck on the movie channel, but you are brilliant nonetheless."

On Saturday Grant comes over in the afternoon to work on our science project. Unfortunately, I have spent so much time focusing on my own science project that I have let the one for Mr. Evans' class slide a bit. I still have a good two weeks to get everything done, but it will still be tight since Grant is only mildly helpful. My plan was to wait until we were done studying to make the grand invitation to Thanksgiving at the Dilts house, but after about twenty minutes my nervousness gets the best of me.

"Grant, there is something I have to ask you."

"If this is about that formula, I told you I don't have any idea what you are talking about."

"No. It's not about that. It's . . . well," I pause for a second. I'm so nervous and I don't even know why. I just need to follow the next step on my list of procedures. I should be as nervous doing this as I would be filling a test tube with hydrogen peroxide. Actually I should be less nervous as there is little chance of causing a volatile chemical reaction. But when I look at Grant just looking at me waiting for my question, I wonder if there is some other type of chemical reaction going on. I put the thought out of my mind.

"Grant, I would really like you to get to know my parents better. I want you to come to Thanksgiving dinner at my house next week with my family. I think it's time they finally got a chance to get to know you." I say the words as quickly as possible. I know he won't dump me just after hearing this. I'll need to push him a bit, beg him to come, and maybe even throw a mild tantrum.

I prepare myself for the drama that is about to unfold when I hear Grant say, "Okay. What time?"

I roll my eyes and look upward. If I had been working at NASA in the sixties we would have landed on a hunk of cheese instead of the moon. Of course he said yes. This guy never does what I expect. He is like a mutant strain of bacteria resistant to all forms of penicillin.

"We usually eat around four," I say with a sigh. I mean, why fight it at this point. I can't believe he doesn't have to check with his parents first. My parents would go through the roof if I suggested spending a holiday anywhere other than home. "Don't you want to check with your mom?"

"Don't need to."

"Are you sure?"

"Yeah, I'm sure," he says, avoiding direct eye contact with me.

"Well, they might want you home for the holiday," I suggest.

"Don't worry about it," he says. It almost seems like his face is getting a bit red.

"Grant, I would understand if—"

Grant slams his fist on his book. "My parents aren't even gonna be here. They're gonna be with my brother and his fiancée on some stupid cruise in some stupid country." Grant takes a second to calm down. I want to say something to him to make him feel better, but I have no idea what to say. I want to say that I think it's awful that his parents would leave him alone on Thanksgiving. I want to say that I'm sorry to have gotten him upset. I want to say a lot of things to him, but instead I don't say anything. I just watch as he puts his stuff in his backpack and walks out the door. "I'll see you Thursday," he says without turning around to look at me.

CHAPTER

25

"Two truths cannot contradict one another."
—Galileo

Thanksgiving is a very special holiday for my family. My mother goes all out preparing side dishes while my father is responsible for deep-frying the turkey outside. One year he nearly burned the house down back in Rancho. My mother has tried to gently suggest that she cook the turkey in the oven this year since they just started paying the mortgage on the new house and are on relatively good terms with the neighbors. My father has promised my mother that the mishap of a few years ago was due to operator error and that he has revised part of his procedural order so that there is little chance of having a repeat of the Flying Turkey Fireball of '03.

I was nervous about asking my parents about having Grant over for dinner. I never thought in a million years he would actually say yes, so I didn't even consider checking with my parents to see if it would be okay. Once Grant accepted I couldn't very well say to him that I changed my mind, so one night after dinner I gathered my courage and asked them. Of course they wanted to know why Grant wasn't having dinner with his family and if I considered Grant to be my boyfriend. Explaining that Grant's parents are on a cruise was easy; explaining if Grant is my boyfriend was much harder. I mean, most of the kids at Greenview think Grant is my boyfriend and certainly Grant's mother thinks I am Grant's girlfriend. Does that alone make us boyfriend-girlfriend?

Dixie, I think, would certainly like it if I did really think about Grant as my boyfriend. He keeps asking me why I don't, and I keep telling him that a good scientist does not get involved with the materials of the experiment in that way. I have very specific reasons for doing what I am doing, and I'm not about to let my feelings for Grant get in the way.

Not that I have feelings for Grant, I remind myself. When we are alone, I see a side of Grant that the other kids at

Greenview might not see, but when Grant is at school in front of his friends, he is still the same Grant that teased me on the first day of school, the same Grant who slacks off in class and has scorned every member of the Holly Trinity. I'm thinking about this as I set the table in the dining room. Mom and Gary are in the kitchen making some last-minute preparations, and my Dad has gone over to pick up Grant. When I hear his car drive up, I get a nervous pit right in the center of my stomach. Maybe I should have taken back my invitation. What if Grant acts like a jerk at dinner? What if he is rude to my parents? What if he shows up wearing his torn jeans and a ripped T-shirt?

My dad opens the door and says, "Gobble. Gobble. Look what the turkey dragged in." Oh God. I totally forgot about being embarrassed by parents. "Make yourself at home, Grant. I need to check on our turkey preparations." My dad walks down the hallway leaving me alone with Grant in the entryway.

Grant is wearing a jacket and tie. His usual mop of blond hair has been neatly tamed by some type of styling product. His cheeks are red like he just scrubbed them in the shower. He looks at me and smiles his most charming grin.

"You look nice," he says. I'm so busy looking at how nice

he looks that I don't even remember what I'm wearing. I look down at myself and quickly realize that I am wearing one of the dresses I bought way back in September at the mall. It's a green wraparound dress with a small floral print. Holly has the exact same dress in light blue.

"Thank you," I say. There are a few seconds of silence. I'm not sure what I should say, and to be honest I'm just enjoying staring at him.

My mom comes in and I snap to attention like she has caught me doing something I should not be doing. "Hi, Grant. Nice to see you again. Dorie tells me you have made some improvements to my minitaco recipe."

"Well, not really improvements, just some changes. The ones you made were awesome."

"What's this?" my mom asks, pointing to the large bag in Grant's hand that I have yet to even realize he is holding.

"Oh, I hope you don't mind. I've been playing around with a few recipes that I thought I could bring over," Grant says.

"Mind? I can't wait to see what you have come up with. Come in the kitchen with me. Dorie, would you check on your father? There's a fire extinguisher in the mudroom." Grant looks a little frightened when he hears the words "fire extinguisher," yet follows my mom into the kitchen.

I grab the small fire extinguisher and a pair of safety goggles, and head to the backyard, where my father is slowly lowering the turkey into a huge pot of boiling liquid. The whole scene is positively medieval. Gary is watching from behind the railing of the deck. They are both wearing safety goggles as well. We must look like we belong in the geek family hall of fame. Once the entire turkey is submerged, my dad backs away from the contraption and joins Gary and me on the back deck. It's a cool November day but since there is a great deal of sun and no wind it isn't cold. The air just feels crisp and clean.

"Dad, what did you think about Grant when you were driving him over?" I ask.

As soon as Gary hears the name he starts teasing me. "Ooh. Grant. Dorkie's got a boyfriend." Gary starts hugging himself and making kissing noises. When he's this juvenile, it is easy to ignore him.

"Gary, stop it. Why don't you go tell you mother the bird is submerged and everything is okay out here."

"But I want to watch it come out," Gary whines.

"There's plenty of time. Go," my dad says, and Gary leaves us alone.

"Dorie, this Grant seems like a nice boy, very polite, shy."

I try not to laugh out loud, as I think that would be very rude to my father. "Dad, that's just it. At school he isn't very nice, he's never polite, and he is as shy as a peacock during mating season."

"Dorie, sometimes people are like isotopes." I know an isotope is some sort of chemistry term, but I am not exactly sure what it is or what my dad means. "Isotopes are elements that have the same atomic number but different atomic masses," he explains.

"Oh," I say, not sure what he is getting at but still trying to find the connection.

"When you work with an isotope, you think you are getting one thing, but really it all depends on what part of the isotope you are examining. An isotope could be one of many things, just like a person. You think a person is only one thing, but everyone, especially boys Grant's age, are really a mix of different things."

The egg timer my dad has in his shirt pocket rings and interrupts us. "Time to get a temperature reading. Can you send Gary out?" My dad goes back to his deep fryer.

"Sure, Dad," I say, walking back in the house and thinking about the complexity of isotopes.

CHAPTER

"In matters of science, curiosity gratified
begets not indolence, but new desires."
—James Hutton

The Monday after Thanksgiving break all anyone can talk about is the upcoming Winter Wonderland dance. There is even a banner hanging in the middle of the cafeteria with a snowflake countdown. Five paper snowflakes cover up one huge painted snowflake. Each day one snowflake is removed. As I wait in the cafeteria line to get my lunch to bring to the library, I stare at the poster. Am I the only person who notices that three of the five snowflakes are exactly alike? I tried to warn everyone something like this would happen. I can only hope that two of the three clones are removed before any of the other snowflakes.

Dixie was away for the entire Thanksgiving break at his aunt's house somewhere in Maryland, so I haven't had a chance to tell him anything. When I saw him before homeroom, there were too many people around to really get into everything, and Dixie can't really be himself in the halls of the school because one of the older boys might suddenly start picking on him. I've never actually been with Dixie when this has happened, but I've heard rumor of it. I'd love for someone to try to start with him when I'm around. I'd hand out black eyes like a meter maid giving parking tickets.

I get to the library and it is empty as usual. "How was your aunt's?" I ask, handing Dixie my tray so he can take it over the circulation desk.

"My aunt Shuggie's was fine, but I will spare you the details of her oyster and apricot stuffing."

"Eww," I say, my mouth puckering at the very thought of the combination.

"Exactly. Anyway, we didn't happen to have the cutest boy from Greenview at our dinner table."

I know what he means, but I decide not to let him get away with it. "Don't sell yourself short, Dixie Finch."

"Thank you for the compliment and I admit I have a

certain visual flair, but everyone knows Grant could be on the cover of a magazine or the lead singer in some boy band. So, was he rude? Did he burp at the table? Was he trying to watch football while you were eating? Did he even thank your parents for inviting him? Was he so freaked out by the whole thing that he dumped you right there and then?"

"Dixie, one question at a time."

"Our lunch period is only thirty-five minutes long. Start talking!" Dixie says, looking at me like I am about to levitate or something.

"I'm sorry to report that Grant was a perfect gentleman. My mother has even offered to teach him how to make mini-apple-tarts next week."

I tell Dixie the whole story—how Grant was nothing like how he acts at school. He was nice to my family, everyone liked him, and he even prepared his own recipes in order to contribute to the meal. My mom went crazy for his cornbread, and Grant even shot some hoops with Gary after helping everyone with the dishes. Overall, it was a very nice day. Grant was a welcome addition to my family's holiday. I tell Dixie the whole pleasant, yet boring, story. I tell him everything, almost.

I don't tell Dixie about the car ride back to Grant's house.

I don't tell him that after my dad and I said good-bye to Grant and after Grant was already at his door we discovered he had left his hat in the car. I don't tell him that I got out of the car and ran back down the long driveway to give it to him. I don't tell him about the smile on Grant's face when he turned around and saw me holding his red knit ski cap. I don't tell him about the ninety seconds that felt outside of time when we just looked at each other under the moonlit sky, our warm breath visible in the cold night air. I don't tell him that if my dad had honked his horn even a second later I might be telling Dixie an entirely different story today. I don't say any of that, and I imagine that is why Dixie can tell I'm omitting something.

"That's *all* that happened?" Dixie asks, slightly disappointed and slightly suspicious.

"That's all," I say. "Look, I have to get to my English class early today. We're having a quiz on *Wuthering Heights*." I actually feel rather confident about the upcoming quiz, but I know if I stay any longer with Dixie, he'll get the rest of the story out of me. It's not that I'm worried he would tell anybody or make fun of me or anything like that. It's just that . . . well, actually I don't know what it is, and lately I've been feeling this way a lot. For a scientist, not knowing is very painful.

CHAPTER

27

"A likely impossibility is always preferable to
an unconvincing possibility." —Aristotle

I am beginning to think I am too young to handle the
amount of stress I handle. Each day I walk into school
and there is one less snowflake on the giant snowflake in
the cafeteria. I consider sneaking into school in the middle of
the night and hot gluing a few hundred snowflakes over the
dang thing. Last night I dreamed Frosty the Snowman was
chasing me down a canyon, driving a dump truck. Sometimes
I wish my subconscious could be a little subtler.

Today, as I wait in line to get my lunch before going to
the library, I do my best to avoid looking at the snowflakes,
but I can feel their presence looking down at me. Mocking

me. I can almost hear one snowflake saying to the other, "Too bad Dorie couldn't complete her experiment." Part of me wants to rip those smug little snowflakes off the wall. Someone taps me on the shoulder, and without thinking I let the stress of my situation get the best of me and turnaround and snap, "WHAT?"

"Gee. You know they make decaf. Give it a try," Holly says.

"Ohmygod. Holly. I'm so sorry. I didn't know it was you. I'm just . . ."

The delightful and charismatic Ms. McAdams finishes my thought for me. "You're under a lot of stress because the dance is coming up."

"Yes," I say, and nod slowly. See how well she knows me already. It's like we have always been destined to be friends.

"You're worried Grant is gonna dump you just before the big event." This time I don't say anything. I'm not stupid enough to say I'm actually worried Grant *isn't* going to dump me. "Why don't you come have lunch with us today, and we can give you all the dirt on Grant. We're over by the window. We'll save you a seat," Holly says, and walks away.

She asked me to have lunch with her.

She actually came up to me and asked me to have lunch with her and Jenny and Alexis. I will actually carry my tray across the cafeteria and take a seat with them. I can't believe it. I think I'm in shock. I probably am in shock. I should probably go to the school nurse and lie down or something, but I would have to be bleeding out of both ears to miss this opportunity.

"Are you deaf? Two dollars and thirty-five cents," the lunch lady says very slowly to me. I look around and realize my daydreaming has backed up the line past the doors of the cafeteria. I quickly pay and walk across the cafeteria to the Table.

Everyone knows what table is the Table, and everyone knows who sits at the Table. The Holly Trinity reigns from the Table like a monarchy rules from a throne. I walk very slowly. I don't want to trip moments before my arrival. Holly sees me, waves her hand, and pulls out a seat for me.

"So, Dorie, tell us. How's Jerkenstein?" Holly asks with a devilish grin.

"Who?" I ask. Two seconds at the Table and I'm already lost.

"You know," Alexis says, "the Jerk-a-holic. Jerky McJerkenstein."

"The King of the Jerks," Jenny says bitterly.

"Jenny, Alexis," Holly says in a stern tone, "that's enough. Let's not let Grant get the best of us. Dorie, we just want to be there for you when he, you know—"

"Dumps you like a hot potato," Jenny jumps in, unable to control herself.

"We were just wondering if he has given you all the warning signs. When he starts acting like a class-A jerk instead of just an average jerk, it means he is about to bolt," Holly warns. I just smile at her. I'm so happy to be sitting at the Table.

This is it.

I'm getting a little sample of what my life will soon be like on a daily basis. Then I realize my continued invitation at this coveted location is seriously in jeopardy. Grant hasn't been acting like more of a jerk. If anything, he has been acting like less of a jerk each time I see him.

"Once," Alexis says, "Grant told me we were going out, but he forgot he had a stupid basketball game so I had to go the game and watch him play. Basketball is sooo boring." The rest of the Trinity members nod their heads and commiserate with Alexis. I don't tell them that I actually enjoyed watching Grant play basketball. Then Jenny tells a story about Grant, then Holly again, and back to Alexis. This continues until the bell rings. I don't really have to say anything for the whole lunch period, and I'm glad because I'm not exactly sure what I would say. The Trinity wishes me luck, and they each gather their purses and book bags. Holly gets up to go to her next class, but before she leaves the table she says to me, "You know, we should all get together and plot some type of revenge against Grant. I mean, of course, once you get dumped." She wiggles her fingers in front of her face in a stylized good-bye, and I smile and try to do the same gesture to each of them.

After they leave I sit at the Table, which once they are gone is just the table, and I can hear Holly's voice in my head: *once you get dumped.* As I get up to go to class, I stare at the maniacal Winter Wonderland dance countdown banner. Darn those snowflakes!

"So, this is where the plebeians eat," Dixie says, entering the side door of the cafeteria. He looks around to make sure almost everyone has cleared out.

"Oh my God. Dixie. I'm sorry. I totally . . ." I am about to say that I forgot about our unofficial lunch appointments in the library, but I stop myself realizing that could hurt his feelings.

"Darlin', I just wanted to make sure you are all right."

"Actually, I'm better than all right. The Holly Trinity asked me to have lunch with them."

Dixie's jaw drops open. "I want to hear everything."

The second warning bell rings. We have just over a minute to get to our next class. "I'll call you tonight," I say.

"I have to go with my mom to help her pick up a new couch from a friend of hers. But I tell you what. I'll bring something really special for lunch for the both of us tomorrow, and you'll fill me in at the library."

"Sounds great," I say, and give Dixie the same finger wave Holly gave me a few minutes earlier.

CHAPTER

"One of the most insidious and nefarious properties of scientific models is their tendency to take over, and sometimes supplant, reality." —Erwin Chargaff

H ey, Dorie," Grant calls before homeroom the next day. I know he knows I hear him, but I still don't turn around. I have been avoiding him all week, and if I'm really being honest with myself, I'm not sure if I've been avoiding him so that he will dump me or so that I don't give him a chance to dump me. I don't think I've ever been so confused in my whole life.

"Dorie," he says, and puts his hand on my shoulder to

turn me around. His face is only a few inches from mine. His deep eyes stare right at me. The halls are crowded, but we might as well be alone in front of his house like we were on Thanksgiving night.

"Yeah?" I say to break the silence.

"Have you gotten any of my e-mails?"

"Ah, sure," I say. The truth is, I haven't checked my e-mail in days. I've been too stressed out.

"Look. The science project is due next week, and we still have to do the conclusion part. Do you want to work on it tonight since we're going to the dance tomorrow?"

"Ah, sure," I say, aware of my temporarily limited vocabulary.

"I'll come over around seven. You okay?"

"Ah, sure," I say, as if I am getting paid by the number of times I say "ah, sure."

"All right," he says, and starts to walk away. Before he turns the corner he adds, "Oh and I sent you the address of the church for my brother's wedding on Saturday. It's Saint Paul's of the Valley over near the old cemetery."

I had totally forgotten about his brother's wedding, not to mention completely forgetting about our project for

Twenty-Eight Great Experiments. Things just seem to be slipping my mind lately.

I put my afternoon books in my locker and slam the door shut when I hear, "Hey, Dorie, I love your sneakers." I turn around and Alexis is pointing at my feet, and Holly and Jenny are smiling. I'm wearing the same white and green sneakers I have worn almost every day since the beginning of the year.

"Thanks," I say.

"We just saw Jerkenstein leave. Did he do it? Did he dump you?" Holly asks.

"No, not yet," I say.

"Hey," Jenny says, "maybe he'll just not show up to the dance like he did with you, Holly."

"Or maybe," Alexis adds, "he'll wait until a few hours before the dance."

"That boy has got some serious problems. Dorie, we'll save you a seat at lunch today. Okay?" I nod my head in agreement. After all, this is what I wanted. Right? "Oh and since you're gonna be in line anyway, can you get each of us a small salad and a diet coke? See ya." Holly leaves, and Jenny and Alexis follow her.

☆ ☆ ☆

As I make my way through the cafeteria trying to balance three salads, three diet cokes, and my own sloppy joe and chocolate milk on one tray, I wonder if this is really what I have been working so hard for. Is this what popularity feels like? Maybe if I can actually get Grant to dump me I'll feel more secure with all of them and the popularity feeling will be more intense or at least more noticeable.

The lunch period passes almost the exact same way it did the day before. Each of them talks about either what they are going to wear to the dance tomorrow, or how much they hate Grant, or what a jerk he is. They laugh at him, call him names, and generally mock him in a way that makes me feel uncomfortable since he is planning on coming over to my house later in the evening. Each of the girls invites me to join in on the bad mouthing, but whenever they do I shove a huge bite of my sloppy joe in my mouth so that I am unable to speak.

During lunch Holly turns to me very seriously and says, "Just because Grant dumps you, doesn't mean you shouldn't go to the dance." Jenny and Alexis pipe in with their agreement. "We'll all be there, and we'll want to hear all about how he dumped you. All right?"

I put the last huge piece of sloppy joe in my mouth
and nod my head. They all get up leaving their half-
eaten salads and empty soda cans behind. Holly glances
back at me and says with a huge smile, "Be a dear and
take those up for us. Thanks."

CHAPTER

29

"The experimenter who does not know what he is looking for will never understand what he finds." —Claude Bernard

Honey, what time is Grant coming over? I wanted to make a copy of a recipe he asked for before he gets here," my mom shouts from the kitchen. I tell her that he is already ten minutes late, and she reminds me that there is some light snow on the road so she is glad whoever is driving him is taking their time.

I use the extra time to review my lab notebook. I carefully read over each part of my experiment to become popular at Greenview, trying to find the moment when it all got out of control. Where exactly did I lose track of the goals of my experiment?

When the doorbell rings, Grant is a full quarter of an hour late. Instead of answering with a pleasant "Hello," I throw open the door and say, "You're late!"

"What's got you in such a bad mood?" Grant asks, wiping some snow from his boots on the doormat. "We were behind a truck that was salting the roads. There was nothing we could do about it."

"Well, we better get started. We have a lot to do. The due date is next week."

"I know that," Grant says. "I'm the one who reminded you."

He's got a point so I don't push it any further. I'm not sure why I am in such a bad mood except for the fact that I am so unsure and that has put me in my present mood.

Grant and I start dividing some of the work that needs to be done. When we first started working together, I never thought I would be able to get him to do a fraction of what we needed to do. Of course, he only volunteers to draw the diagrams and work on the model. He leaves most of the heavy reading and all the writing of the actual report to me.

My mom interrupts us with a plate of cookies. She has taken a real liking to Grant. I think she feels bad for him because his own family has such little interest in him. As soon as she leaves, the phone rings and she comes back to let me know it's for me. Immediately I realize the huge mistake I have made. I run out of the dining room, pick up the phone from my mom, and find my private spot in the hall closet.

"Hello, Dixie?" I say into the phone my voice cracking.

"Well, at least you aren't dead. I just wanted to make sure," he says, his anger sending shockwaves through the phone. I totally forgot about meeting him for lunch. I knew he was planning something special too. It's just that when Holly assumed I would eat with them, I just didn't think. I feel terrible about blowing off Dixie.

"I had lunch with Holly, Jenny, and Alexis."

"I wouldn't be so mad if you at least had a good excuse."

What is he talking about? He knows how important this experiment has been to me. He's helped me with so much of it. How could he not see that this was not only a good reason but an excellent reason?

"Well, maybe after a few lunches with them you'll see what they are really like."

"Dixie, I already see what they are like. They are the most popular girls at school."

"They are the meanest girls at school. They are popular because people are scared of them."

"That's not true," I say, though there is a nagging feeling in the back of my mind that it actually might be true.

"It is true. I thought you were smarter than this, Dorie. I thought you would see that Grant's not such a bad guy, and that the Holly Trinity is meaner than Joan Crawford in *Queen Bee*."

"Dixie—" I say his name and hope I will be able to come up with a comeback, but he cuts me off before I even get a chance to find out.

"Look, Dorie, if being popular is so important to you, then you should just go and finish your experiment."

"Dixie, don't be this way. You are acting like such a jerk!" I shout into the phone.

"I'm acting like a jerk?" Dixie shouts back. Now we are officially fighting. "I don't want anything to do with your experiment anymore. I wash my hands of it. Good-bye!" Dixie slams down the phone. No one has ever hung up on me before. My face is bright red. I don't even know if I'm angry, mad, upset, or hurt. I can actually feel the blood rushing in my face. My ears even tingle. I march back to the dining room, taking my foul mood with me.

I expect to see Grant working on the project, but instead he has folded a piece of paper into a minifootball and is preparing to try and make a field goal over the dining room chairs. "What are you doing?" I scream.

"Just taking a break while you're on the phone."

I grab the paper toy out of his hand. "We don't have time for this. Do something. You can't expect me to do everything."

"What's wrong with you?" Grant asks. I can almost feel tears welling up in my eyes. I quickly move my hand across my face in case there is any sight of them. My anger is about to explode.

"I'll tell you what's wrong with me. I'm tired of doing all the work while you just sit there playing games like an idiot. You are such a dummy!" I actually call him a dummy. As soon as the word comes out of my mouth I know I shouldn't have said it. Now Grant's face is just as red as mine, but he isn't angry or mad—he is just hurt. He puts his hand to his face and I wonder if he is doing that to avoid showing any tears. What have I done?

"Well," he says, "I may not be a genius or even very smart.

Maybe I don't want everyone to know that I have problems in school because I can't read that good, but I'm NOT a dummy." Now he is getting angry. I want to apologize. I want to ask for his forgiveness but he is too worked up. "I'm smart enough to have figured out your whole plan for using me."

Oh no. I quickly look down at the ground. I can't bear to make eye contact with him. He digs under a pile of papers and pulls out my lab notebook.

"I saw this while you were on the phone. I saw all your notes on Holly, Jenny, and Alexis."

I snatch the book from his hands. "That is private."

"I thought it was part of the project when I opened it, but then I read through it. You were just using me to get in with those girls, what you call the Holly Trinity."

"How dare you go through my private things." I really have no defense, so I just yell back at him with the one piece of evidence I can possibly use to defend myself.

"The thing is, Dorie, I thought you were different. You weren't like those girls. You seemed . . ." Grant looks at my notebook again and just the act of looking at it seems to bring back his anger. "You want to know why I broke up with each of them? Because they are selfish, shallow, and mean. You'll fit in with them perfectly."

Grant grabs his backpack off the table and heads out of the dining room. "You want your experiment to work so badly. You want me to dump you?" Grant pulls open the front door and a gust of cold wind with some snow blows in. "Well, Dorie, consider yourself dumped!" He leaves and slams the door behind him.

CHAPTER

30

"Every student who enters upon a scientific
pursuit, especially if at a somewhat
advanced period of life, will find not only
that he has much to learn, but much also to
unlearn." —John Frederick William Herschel

On Friday I walk around school like a zombie.
Dixie won't return my calls or e-mails. I think
he is just too mad to even talk to me. I look for
him in the halls in between classes hoping to run into him,
but I have no luck. I am too humiliated even to look at
Grant. However, this doesn't seem to be an issue since he
makes sure he is not within ten yards of me the entire day.
I can't go to the library to eat my lunch, and I can't bear

to have the Holly Trinity see me so upset. I buy a sandwich and quickly walk to the girls' room I sat in way back in the beginning of the year when I was gathering my data on the Holly Trinity. I sit in the familiar spot and try to pull myself together. I'm hoping that returning to the origin of the hypothesis will somehow inspire me.

I play with the wrapper of my sandwich and remind myself that I have finally gotten what I've wanted. When I show up alone at the dance tonight I will finally be popular. Why in the world would I be upset about this? Was Edison upset when he discovered the light bulb? Was Marie Curie upset when she discovered radiation? Did Jane Goodall sit on her bed on the verge of tears when she discovered tool use among chimpanzees?

Two hours before the dance I'm lying on my bed in my room just staring at the ceiling. I pictured this night so differently. I thought I would be so excited to get ready. I imagined carefully doing my hair and makeup, maybe even with Dixie's help. I imagined talking on the phone with Holly and getting fashion advice from Alexis. I get up from my bed to get ready. I pass by my bookshelf and notice my *Encyclopedia of Great Scientists*. Since I am not that anxious to get ready for the dance, I plop back down on the bed with the book, and it randomly opens to the biography of Alexander Fleming.

Oh my God! Of course. I can't believe I hadn't considered this earlier.

Alexander Fleming, the scientist who discovered penicillin, did so quite by accident. He noticed that mold spores had contaminated a bacteria sample left by an open window. Most scientists would have just thrown out the spoiled sample, but Fleming took a closer look at it and discovered that the mold was actually killing the bacteria. A few test tubes later and he turns his mistake into one of the greatest scientific discoveries of all time—penicillin.

A good scientist takes into account all aspects of an experiment, the good and the bad. I started off with one goal, but my experiment has allowed me to discover something else entirely. I can't believe I have been so blind.

I run downstairs and grab the phone off the wall to call Grant.

His phone rings twice and then his voice mail picks up. I know he is screening his calls. The dance is in less than two hours. There is still a chance this will work out. I should hang up, take out a piece of paper, and write down exactly what I should say, but instead when I hear the beep I just start speaking extemporaneously.

"Hi, Grant. It's Dorie. I know what I did was awful, and I didn't even apologize for it, and that is even more awful than the actual thing I did. I wanted to say I'm sorry. I'm sorry for everything. You are a really great guy, and I've had a great time getting to know you these past few months, and I'm sorry I couldn't see what was in front of my eyes. Look, I would still love to go to the dance with you. Meet me at six fifteen on the side entrance to the multipurpose room. I hope I see you there." I hang up. I hope that was enough to convince him to meet me. I run back upstairs to my room. My enthusiasm for getting ready for the dance has been restored.

My dad drops me off at school at exactly 6:05 p.m. On the way over he gives me some speech about boy-girl relationships. I nod a lot and say uh-huh, but I'm not really listening to any of it. I am too focused on praying that Grant meets me outside the multipurpose room. It takes me two minutes to get from the car to the spot at the side door I said I would be at. I don't see Grant anywhere. I can see a bunch of kids going in the main doors from where I am. By 6:12 I begin to get more nervous. I can feel my heart pounding. I remind myself that Grant can be a little tardy sometimes, so when 6:15 comes and goes I try not to get too upset. By 6:25, however, I feel pretty discouraged. I don't see any sign of Grant. At 6:33 I decide to give up. There is a pay phone on the other side of the gym. I'll call my dad and have him come pick me up.

I try to walk quickly past the main entrance to the dance. I don't even want to look inside. I just want to go home. Maybe Dixie has finally decided to return my calls.

"Dorie! Dorie!" I hear just when I thought I have made it safely to the other side of the door. I don't have to turn around to see who it is. It's Holly. A month ago the very thought of her even acknowledging my existence would have thrilled me. Now I could care less.

The Holly Trinity runs out of the dance to talk to me.

"So, we see you're here alone. I guess that idiot finally dumped you. I knew he would," Holly says. Her voice is so smug.

"Grant is such a loser," Jenny says.

"A total loser," Alexis adds.

"Actually," I say, my voice deadly serious, "Grant is a great guy."

All three of them laugh out loud as if I have told the world's funniest joke.

"Great guy?" Holly mocks. "Maybe if you like dating someone who has the IQ of a cardboard box. Grant is a total dummy."

That's it. I can't take one more second of their bad-mouthing Grant. "You are the one who is a dummy if you can't see how great a guy Grant is. You are shallow and mean, and the only reason you think you are so popular is because most of the kids are just scared of you. You aren't well-liked, you are feared. All three of you."

My outburst has almost no effect on them. Each of them rolls their eyes and laughs. They just walk away, taking any chance I ever had of being popular with them.

Then from the other end of the hall coming from the darkness I hear someone clapping. First the person claps slowly one beat at a time, but as the clapping gets closer the tempo gets quicker. I think the person might be clapping for me.

"Well done, darlin', well done."

"DIXIE!" I shout, and give him a big hug. As soon as he hugs me back I know everything with us will be all right.

"Dixie, I'm sorry about not listening to you and about taking you for granted."

He studies me very closely. I wonder if some stray zipper is open or something.

"And what else are you sorry for?"

There are probably a hundred things I should be sorry for, but I can't seem to think of one at the moment. Dixie looks at me with fake anger and grabs my hands.

"What about these, Miss Dorie?" Oh, God. I suddenly remember that I have forgotten to remember to stop biting my nails. The polish that Dixie painstakingly applied under a week ago is chipped and the nails are rough and uneven. "I didn't spend the better part of my lunch hour giving a fabulous manicure just to see my artwork treated this way." He is smiling as he says it, so I know he is only teasing.

"And I'm sorry for treating the best and only manicure I've ever had so shabbily. I promise it'll never happen again."

"Okay. You're forgiven," Dixie says, and just like that we are back to being friends. "Now let's go see how my fabulous ideas for decorations turned out, shall we?"

He holds out his arm and we walk in the main entrance together. The multipurpose room has been transformed. Soft white lights flicker from beneath fake snowdrifts made of cotton. The beaded icicles that Dixie created glisten under the soft lights, and there are hundreds of paper snowflakes hanging. It truly looks like a Winter Wonderland.

I notice a few of the kids are dancing in the center of the room. No one is really in couples—everyone is just moving to the music and having a good time. "Let's dance," Dixie says.

"Dixie," I say with a big smile, "this is very Julia Roberts and Rupert Everett in *My Best Friend's Wedding*, don't you think?" I know my cinematic reference will create quite a reaction.

"OH MY GOD! Darlin', you actually watched a movie. Can a daily facial moisturizing routine be that far behind?" Dixie pretends to sob with joy as he enters the dance floor. He always makes me laugh no matter how rotten I feel.

As we join everyone else on the dance floor I realize that my experiment actually yielded exactly what I wanted. I thought I wanted to be popular, to have a group that I fit in with. What I really wanted was a friend, a good friend. When I look at the fashionably dressed guy dancing with himself not caring who's looking at him, I realize I've found one.

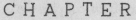

CHAPTER

"Science says the first word on everything,
and the last word on nothing." —Victor Hugo

My dad is always telling me that a good scientist has a tidy lab. "Just because you've discovered plutonium doesn't mean you can throw your lab coat on the floor," he'll say. I'm not actually sure this is sound scientific advice. It is more likely a ploy of his to get me to clean my room. Regardless, I have taken it to heart. There is still one loose end of my experiment, and I plan to tie that up.

The morning after the dance I get up early and put on my best most formal outfit: a deep blue velvet dress with ribbon trim that I wore to my cousin's wedding last year.

It actually fits better than it did last year since I can fill it out more in some of the more important places.

I have the address of the church where they are having Grant's brother's wedding in my e-mail, and my dad has said he would drop me off. I didn't really explain why Grant's family wasn't picking me up. I think he assumed they were too busy with the preparations to have one more detail to take care of.

As we get closer to the church I get more nervous. Grant didn't show up at the dance last night. Maybe he wants nothing to do with me. I should have at least called him to let him know I was coming. Maybe I should just tell my dad I forgot something at home and then run to my bedroom and lock myself in the bathroom. As we get closer and closer to the church, that sounds like a better and better idea. I'm about to tell my dad to drive back when he pulls up to the side of the church and reminds me to call home if I need anything. It's too late to turn back.

I get out of the car and wave good-bye to my dad. I'm wearing my mom's cashmere wrap but the cold winter morning air still gives me a chill. I walk toward the side door of the church even though I notice most people are going through the main entrance. I figure I'll just warm up for a second before going in. I also need to think of a plan for what I am going to say to Grant. I've been racking my brain trying to think of something, but nothing has come to me.

I open the small door and the warmth of the church embraces me. I take off the shrug and place it on the bench next to me. There is a thick red velvet curtain between where I am standing in the vestibule and the main part of the church. I make sure the door is shut and move closer to the curtain to stay warm. I can hear muffled voices on the other side of the curtain. As soon as I do, I recognize the calm, mellifluous voice of Mrs. Bradish, Grant's mother. At least now I know I'm at the right church. I move a few inches closer to see if I can make out what she is saying. Maybe Grant is with her.

"Grant, stop slouching," she says to him, her tone stern and even. "This a very important day for your brother. I hope you can understand that."

"Yes, Mom," Grant says. The sound of his voice makes all of my nervous energy return. I do my best to remain calm.

"It's bad enough I told all of my friends and your brother's future in-laws that you would be here with a girl, and now I have to explain why you are here alone. It's always something with you to try to get attention."

"Yes, Mom," Grant says. My heart breaks for him.

"I should have known. That girl was just too smart for you," Mrs. Bradish says. I take that as my cue.

"Actually, Mrs. Bradish," I say, pushing back the heavy velvet curtain to reveal myself, "I think Grant is too smart for *me*. I wasn't able to find the right church. Sorry to be so late, Grant." Grant just looks at me. I can identify shock and relief on his face, and it doesn't seem like there is much anger there, so I take this as a good sign.

"Wonderful," Mrs. Bradish sighs. "I'm going to make sure your brother is doing all right." She walks away and the back of her gown floats behind her. Grant and I are alone.

"I hope you don't mind me showing up like this," I say.

"No, I don't mind," he says, looking down at his shoes. "I heard you stood up for me at the dance."

"Word travels fast around here," I say, surprised that he found out so quickly.

"Yeah, Doug called me last night. Well, thanks for . . . ," he says.

"Grant, I'm sorry for everything."

"Dorie, I thought about it, and you really didn't do anything wrong. I should be apologizing. I was such a jerk to you when we first met. I guess I was intimidated or something."

"Well, I guess we're even," I say.

"I guess so," Grant says, looking up from the floor for the first time. The church organ begins to play, signaling that we should take our seats. "This way," he says, holding out his arm.

"Oh wait," I say. "I left my wrap in the vestibule."

"I'll get it," he says, and goes behind the curtain to retrieve it. I push back the heavy curtain and follow him.

On the other side of the curtain the organ music is muted yet more intense. A small cold wind sneaks in from a crack in the window next to the door. A cloud passes in front of the sun, making the vestibule much darker than it was earlier.

"There it is," I say, pointing to the bench. Grant picks it up and says, "Let me help you with this." He holds the wrap open and I turn around so he can place it on my shoulders. Then I make another half turn to finish. This places me directly in front of him. We stand face to face. His eyes look deep into mine. My heart is racing. I pray my ears are not burning red.

"This reminds me of standing in front of my house Thanksgiving night," he says.

"Me too," I say, because it does remind me of that night. I have the same intense feeling I had then.

"Maybe," Grant says, "I can do now what I wanted to do then."

I know exactly what he is going to do. All of my not knowing has evaporated. I slowly nod my head and my eyes close as if by instinct. The next thing I feel are Grant's lips on my lips. He kisses me softly. It only lasts a few seconds, but it feels much longer. The organ music swells and we pull apart at the exact same time. I rest my forehead on his chin for just a moment.

"We better get to our seats," he whispers into my ear.

During the ceremony we sit side by side in one of the front pews. At one point Grant lets his hand drop from his lap to his side and it lands on top of mine. My initial reaction is to move my hand out of the way, but Grant gently squeezes my hand in his and smiles at me, so I keep it exactly where it is.

That night, after the wedding reception, before I go to sleep I take out my lab notebook. I promised myself that I would fill out the conclusions for my experiment before I went to bed. I stare at the perfect grid created by the intersecting lines of the graph paper and try to remember everything that has happened over the past few months. The truth is, I am no more popular now than I was back in September. But science isn't always about getting results; sometimes it just helps you see the world from a different perspective.

Dorie Dilts—Lab Report—FINAL DRAFT
Conclusions: To be continued.

Dorie Dilts's

Partial Thermal Degradation of Carbon Dioxide Foamed Saccharides with Protein Inclusions
(Peanut Brittle)

MATERIALS:

Sucrose (Sugar)

Glucose solution (Corn syrup)

H_2O (Water)

Solidified esters (Butter)

Sodium chloride (Salt)

Protein pellets (Peanuts)

Sodium bicarbonate (Baking soda)

4-hydroxy-3-methoxy-benzaldehyde (Vanilla)

Aluminum foil

Jelly roll pan

Thermometer

Cooking pot

Spoon

Hot plate or stove

PROCEDURE:

1. Mass out the following materials and set aside: 9.5g of solidified esters, 0.3g of sodium chloride, 60g of protein pellets, 3.5g of sodium bicarbonate, and 1.3 mL of 4-hydroxy-3-methoxy-benzaldehyde.
2. Lightly coat the aluminum foil with the .5g of solidified esters. Place aluminum foil on jelly roll pan.
3. Mass out the following material and place in cooking pot: 74g of sucrose, 60g of the glucose solution, and 18g of H_2O.
4. Place the thermometer in the cooking pot over medium heat. While stirring constantly, bring to a boil.
5. Add the solidified esters to the boiling mixture.
6. Continue to boil over low heat and stir until the mixture reaches a temperature of 138°C (280°F).
7. When the temperature of the mixture reaches 138°C (280°F) add the sodium chloride and the protein pellets. Continue to stir.
8. When the temperature of the mixture reaches 154°C (309°F), remove from heat. Remove the thermometer. Stir vigorously while adding the sodium bicarbonate

and the 4-hydroxy-3-methoxy-bensaldehyde. Chemical reaction will occur.

9. Stir for about 1 minute and then pour the mixture on the coated aluminum foil. Let cool. Break into smaller specimens.

NOTE: This experiment is for advanced scientists or scientists who are working in cooperation with a senior lab technician or parental unit.

Dorie's back with a new social experiment!
Here's a peek at the next Dorie Dilts novel,

The School
for Cool

CHAPTER

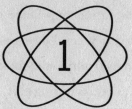

1

"Somewhere, something incredible is waiting
to be known." —Carl Sagan

Science has figured out how far a single beam of
light can travel in one year, and yet, how long it
takes a single letter to get from Washington, D.C.
to Greenview, New Jersey, is still a mystery. I am trying to
forget the fact that my entire summer will be decided by
a letter that may or may not be waiting in my mailbox
when I get home from school today. It would be so amazing if we both get in. I don't know what I'll do if I get in
and Dixie doesn't or if Dixie gets in and I don't.

I take a bite of my turkey sandwich, hoping it will

distract me. Dixie and I are eating lunch in our usual spot in the library. I actually enjoy eating lunch behind the circulation desk. I started meeting Dixie here at the beginning of school last year when I developed my experiment to infiltrate the Holly Trinity—the most popular clique at school. Dixie shelves books during part of his lunch period so that he can avoid getting teased in the testosterone-laden lunchroom. At first I was terrified of getting crumbs on some important piece of library material, but Dixie taught me to not worry so much about that—as well as teaching me some other important lessons. I guess that's what a best friend is for.

I look over at Dixie, who is staring at me as he nibbles on a mini-sushi roll that he delicately holds with a pair of chopsticks. He can tell I am still preoccupied.

"Dorie, the application said the letter will arrive on or about the first of June," Dixie says.

"Well, today is May thirty-first, so in my book, that is on or about the first of June," I tell him. "How can you be so calm?"

"Dorie, dearie, I'm as nervous as you are, but we both promised that if either of us didn't get in, we would not get upset. *Que sera, sera, chérie.*"

We actually made this pact at the Greenview post office when we sent off our applications to the National Academy for Gifted Youth (return-receipt requested). We found out about the program one winter morning when Principal Wabash made an announcement that students interested in applying for the nation's most prestigious summer youth enrichment program could pick up applications in the main office. Dixie and I each picked up a brochure and application—mine for the Science Academy and his for the Arts Academy. The brochure said that each summer, the nation's top middle-grade students spend eight weeks studying the field of their choice with college faculty from around the country.

"Oh my God," I said as I clutched my brochure.

"What's wrong?" Dixie asked.

"It says here that last year the science students worked on co-vinyl acetates."

"So?"

"Well, I've only been interested in acetates since I was like ten!" Dixie just looked at me.

"I might have more of a reaction if I actually knew what an acetate was."

"Oh, an acetate is just a chemical compound that—"

I started to explain, but Dixie put his finger to my lips.

"Shh. Let it remain in my little treasure chest of scientific mysteries for which you alone hold the key." I laughed out loud. Dixie always cracks me up.

"Anyway, listen to this: Last year the Arts Academy did a full production of *Gypsy,* which they presented on one of the stages at the Kennedy Center."

"Wow," I sighed. "*Gypsy* and acetates, an embarrassment of riches."

That night Dixie and I began working on our applications. We had to submit grades, letters of recommendation, and an essay explaining a project we would work on at that summer. Every day during lunch we would read over our applications with each other. After we mailed them off we actually forgot about them until about a month ago, when I realized the decision letters were due to be mailed out.

Just then the bell signaling the end of the lunch period rings, and we grab our backpacks. As we leave the library I instruct Dixie, "Now if you get a letter when you get home from school, call me."

"I call you every day after school anyway," Dixie says as he takes a pair of large vintage sunglasses out of his bag and places them on the top of his head.

"Aren't those supposed to go over your eyes?" I ask.

"If you put them on your eyes, they're glasses. If you put them on the top of your head, they're an accessory," Dixie says, and walks across the hall, melting into the afternoon pedestrian traffic at Greenview Middle School. I start heading toward my English class when I hear a voice coming at me from down the hall.

"Hey, Dorie. Dorie." I turn around and there's Grant, smiling and waving at me. His blond hair flops in his face a bit as his lithe body makes its way though the crowd of kids in the hall. The thought of having to said good-bye to Grant for the whole summer is the only thing that makes the possibility of getting accepted bittersweet. On the other hand, there is a chance that the time apart will be good for us. Dixie insisted that Grant is my boyfriend, although Grant has never actually called himself my *boyfriend* and I have never called myself his *girlfriend*. After we first kissed at his brother's wedding way back in December, he went away with his family to some mountain resort in the Alps for the holidays, and didn't come back until the middle of January. We e-mailed each other a few times, and when he got back to school we were definitely more than friends, but I was not exactly sure if we were officially going out.

☆ ☆ ☆

This afternoon, I get so caught up trying to figure out my relationship with Grant that I barely think about the possibility of getting my NAGY acceptance letter until I am walking home. As I turn the corner I see the white postal truck slowly crawling down my street. It's already a few houses down the block from mine. I run to the mailbox in front of our house and check for the letter.

The mailbox is empty. How is that possible? We always get something in the mail. At the very least my mom gets some catalog or a coupon for a free bikini wax or something.

I shut the the mailbox door and chase after the postal truck. It goes very slowly, so even though it is a few houses away, it is easy to catch.

"Mr. Vernhart, excuse me, but is there a chance that you skipped our house today? Because there was no mail in our mailbox, and I'm expecting . . ."

"You're expecting a very important letter." Mr. Vernhart, with whom I have developed a close if not stalkerlike relationship since mailing out my NAGY application, finishes my sentence for me. "I know, so I hand-delivered your mail right to your front door today," he says.

"Oh my God. Thank you. Thank you," I say, running as fast as I can back to my house. By the time I open the back door, I'm panting. My mother stands in front of me, holding a very official-looking envelope that is addressed to me, Dorie Dilts.

My mom hands me the letter, and I rip it open and read it without even taking off my backpack.

"'Dear Mr. Igor Ellis, we are happy to let you know . . .'" I read the words out loud because I can't believe what I am reading and am not actually sure what it means. "Mom," I ask, hoping she will be able to make some sense of this, "who in the world is Igor Ellis, and why do I have *his* acceptance letter in *my* envelope?"

Judging from my mom's expression, she is as confused as I am. "Dorie, I have no idea."

"Well," I say, "I guess this means I didn't get in. I suppose I could get a part-time job this summer or work on that DNA model I keep telling myself I'm going to build. We should probably get in touch with this Igor Ellis, let him know the big news. I'm sure he'll be very pleased."

I toss the letter on the counter and tell my mom I am

going upstairs to get started on my homework. I promise myself that I will not cry until I am alone in my bedroom. I wanted this so badly. I just hope Dixie gets accepted to the Arts Academy—at least then I will be able to live vicariously through him.

"Hey, Dorie, wait!" my mom says, picking up the letter. "Look! Look at this." She shakes the envelope, and stuck underneath the first letter is another piece of paper.

"It's another letter," my mom says.

"No way," I shout, and charge back into the kitchen.

"Here. Here. Read it," my mom says, handing it to me.

"'Dear Ms. Dorie Dilts . . .'"